THE THREE MYSTERIOUS TALES

RICKO DUPRI SAMPLE

Tellwell Talent
www.tellwell.ca

ISBN
978-0-2288-0829-9 (Paperback)

About the Author

About the Author: At fourteen, Ricko Dupri Sample is currently in his second year of college. He works as a model and actor and lives with his family in Auburn, Washington. *Bigfoot Untold* was his first book.

About the Book

About the Book: Read three tales of the journeys and the experiences of different people, each being mysterious and odd in their own way. In the first tale, a sixteen-year-old girl, along with her roommates and friends, witness the magical power of a well in a town called Green Mountain. In the second tale, a twenty-five-year-old woman listens to stories about mysterious circumstances related to crocodiles while living in the city of Victorious. In the third tale, two brothers each experience their own, odd hunting encounter in the wilderness of Bitterfruit and Jungletown.

Table of Contents

A Different Well..1

1. The Beginning 3
2. The Well's Water 15
3. A Ghostly Visitor 26
4. Taking Advantage 35

Bizarre Reptiles.. **41**

1. Released & Returned...........................43
2. The Fisherman & The Crocodile.........49

Hunting Encounters **57**

1. Double Brother 59
2. Jerry & Layla 68

Afterword 97

A DIFFERENT WELL

I

The Beginning

A sixteen-year-old girl in high school named Shelly lived in a town, with her roommates Ruby, Lisa, and Jessica. Shelly was the youngest. She never wore a skirt. She simply liked to wear pants or shorts, and her hair was wavy and always short like a tomboy. She was shy and soft-spoken around people, especially people she didn't know well. Despite being more of a tomboy, she didn't act as wild as other tomboys in her town. The rest of her roommates were older and were college students.

Ruby and Lisa were quite the opposite of Shelly. Ruby's hair was straight and above her shoulders. She and Lisa acted more like *girly girls*. They usually wore skirts and high heels when going to college. Lisa, however, was taller than Ruby. Lisa's hair was similar to Ruby's hair, but Lisa's was wavy. They're both outgoing and a bit talkative. Jessica was childish and fun. Her hair was above her shoulders and also curly. She sometimes wore a skirt, sometimes she simply wore jeans.

The town they lived in was called Scarcetree, and it was located in Washington State. This town was always crowded, especially in the day time. It mostly consisted of a metropolitan area, although there was a small, industrialized suburban area on the outskirts of the city. The majority of school students who lived there were college students. The houses were close to each other, and they didn't have backyards. There was a large sports stadium in the downtown area. There were several colleges nearby the suburban area. The city had hospitals, hotels, several thriving businesses, apartments, restaurants, a post office, and an international airport. Across the street of Shelly's house was a factory that produced plastic.

The house was one-story, but large. It had six bedrooms, two bathrooms, and one living room. The house also had a big dining room and kitchen. Shelly and her roommates rented a room, except Ruby. Ruby was the owner's daughter. Shelly lived in this house because it was nearby her school. Her school was only fifteen minutes away on foot. Her family lived three hours away in a small town somewhere near a city called Dogwood.

One early Friday afternoon in late spring of 2005, a young man named Jack was talking with Lisa on the porch. Jack was a tall and outgoing young man. His hair was curly and short. Jack lived with his parents, next door to his grandfather, Mr. Johnson. Jack didn't go to college and had a job. His job was nearby the shore. He could enter Mr. Johnson's house through a kitchen door connected to his grandfather's kitchen, since their houses were connected to each other.

Shelly was rushing to her room after school when Lisa saw her.

"Shelly, why are you in a hurry?"

"I'm going home."

"Oh," said Lisa, disappointed. "Jack and I are going to the ocean tomorrow near where Jack works, and then from there we're gonna go to my house. We thought you might want to come."

"I'm running out of money," Shelly said. "I have to pay rent and my phone bill."

"You can just call your parents," said Jack, "and ask them to send you some money."

"Yeah," said Lisa. "I do it all the time when I am unable to go home."

Shelly smiled and took a deep breath. "That's a good idea. Okay then."

So, later that evening, she was going to get some food with her roommate Lisa at a nearby restaurant. On the way there, Lisa asked Shelly something.

"Hey Shelly, have you called your parents, yet?"

"I did try to call my parents, but I found out that my phone got temporarily cut off, since I didn't pay my phone bill."

"Oh, you could use my phone."

"Can I use it now?"

"You have to wait until we get home. I don't have it on me right now."

"Well never mind, it's alright," Shelly said. "There is a telephone booth at the restaurant. I can just call them from there. Thank you for offering me your phone, though."

"Alright, it's no problem."

And so when they reached the restaurant, Shelly went over to the phone booth. However, when she called, no one was home to pick up the phone, and so she left a message.

"Hi Mom and Dad, sorry I missed you. I'm calling because I ran out of money, and I can't come home. Please send me money soon, I love you."

Unfortunately, her parents didn't have the house's phone number and Shelly's cellphone had been cut off, so they couldn't call her back.

Her parents started worrying.

Next week, on a Thursday, after she got off school, she was sitting on her porch. One of her roommates, Jessica, came and sat beside her.

"Are you going home this coming weekend?"

"No," Shelly said. "I was supposed to go home last week, but Lisa and Jack told me not to go home and told me to just call my parents to send me some money so that I can go to the ocean and then head to Lisa's house."

"Oh okay," Jessica said. "By the way, I met your brother and mother last Monday."

"Yes, I saw them then as well."

"Oh, good. I didn't know if you'd talked to them. I had to go to my classes and when I came home, it was already late."

"Yeah, they didn't stay for long."

Last Monday, Shelly's brother and mother went to visit Shelly. They were asking people around if they knew who Shelly was. They were trying to find out where she was when they ran into Jessica.

Shelly's brother, named Tony, introduced himself to her. "Hi, my name is Tony. I'm trying to find a person named Shelly. I'm Shelly's brother and this is my mom, Casey."

"Oh hi, nice to meet you. I'm Jessica, Shelly's roommate."

She then shook Tony's and his mother's hands. Tony was of average height and build. He had short and wavy hair and was a laid-back individual who didn't talk a lot. He normally didn't laugh and usually just smiled.

Tony and his mother were pleased to meet her.

"Do you know where Shelly is?" Tony asked.

"Yes, she's still in school."

From out of the blue, there was a law student named Larry. He liked Shelly, but he was a lot older than her. Shelly didn't like him back, however. He overheard Shelly's mother and brother speaking to Jessica, so he came to introduce himself to them.

"Hi, my name is Larry. I live next door to Shelly."

Shelly's brother and then his mother shook Larry's hand.

"Nice to meet you, Larry. I'm Tony and this is my mom."

Then, Johnson came out.

"Oh," said Jessica, "here is the owner of our house. Hi, Mr. Johnson, this is Shelly's mother and brother. I've gotta go now, I need to head to my classes."

"Okay," Tony said. "It was nice talking to you, have a nice day."

"Thank you, you too."

Casey waved good-bye.

Mr. Johnson allowed them to come in and sit in his living room. Mr. Johnson was an old and friendly man, around seventy-five years old, who had live there for years. He allows college students to rent the rooms in his house, especially for women. This is because only one of his daughters Ruby and his wife Katherine lived with him, and the house was very large. He was not really active, so he mostly stayed in his bedroom. He had five kids, and Ruby was the youngest. All of his kids had gotten married and had their own houses except Ruby. She was still in college.

Mr. Johnson's wife, Katherine, was around fifteen years younger than Mr. Johnson; however, that didn't stop her from being a hard worker. She was energetic and busy. She had a shop near a market a mile away from the house. Every weekday, she left at five in the morning and came home late in the afternoon, at around four. When she got home, she mostly just rested in her room. Ruby did most of the work at home.

"Come on in and make yourself comfortable," Mr. Johnson said, "and you too, Larry. Accompany them."

"Thank you, sir."

Tony and his mother thanked him too.

They entered the house, and Mr. Johnson went back to his room. As Larry, Tony, and his mother were having a conversation, Ruby came in.

"Hi Ruby, meet Shelly's mom and her brother."

They all introduced themselves.

"Shelly is still in school," Ruby said, "But I can go tell her that you're here."

"Oh, no need," said Shelley's mom "We'll be waiting right here until she comes, thank you though."

"It is fine. I can still go to her school and tell her that you're waiting."

Ruby left to go to Shelly's school. Not too long later, Shelly arrived at the house. There she saw Larry sitting and chatting with her mother and brother. Shelly didn't want to enter the house until Larry left. Larry saw Shelly outside the house through the window. He just saw her waiting there.

He decided that she was waiting for him to leave.

"I have to go now. Goodbye, Tony and Casey. It was nice to meet you."

He shook Tony's and Casey's hands. They said their goodbyes, then Larry went out. When Larry came out, Shelly didn't face him.

Once he'd gone, Shelly went in.

"Mom, why are you here?"

"We were worrying, I thought something was wrong."

"We were all worried," said Tony. "We tried to contact you, but you didn't answer, so Mom decided to come visit to make sure that you were fine."

"Oh, I'm so sorry to trouble you," Shelly said. "My friends wanted me to go with them, so I decided not to go home. I was waiting for some money to be sent by you guys because I couldn't pay my phone bill. I didn't know you had to go through this."

"I'm just glad that you're fine," Casey said. "Your father couldn't sleep last night, and your grandma couldn't eat."

"I'm sorry, Mom. I'll try not to make you worried again."

"...and because of that, I'm going to try to communicate more clearly on the phone when anything happens." Shelly said. "So they don't worry."

Jessica nodded. "I'm sure they'll appreciate that."

"Hey, so I went to the ocean last Saturday and got to see whales. The whale splashed water on us. It was cool, but we all got wet."

"You went with Lisa? Did you go to her house afterward?"

"Yeah."

"How was it?"

"The ocean was nice and calm," Shelly said. "Many boats were there, and we got to ride to one of them and looked at whales. We didn't stay that long because it was too hot. Later on we went to Lisa's house."

"How did you get out there?"

"We took a cab to the ocean, then a bus to get to Lisa's house."

Last Saturday morning at ten o'clock, Jack, Lisa, and, Shelly were on the porch waiting for a cab. When it arrived, it took about thirty minutes to get to the ocean. Shelly was so excited and couldn't wait to get to a boat. Jack knew the people over there.

One of Jack's friends had a boat. His name was Aaron, and he smiled when he saw the three friends. Jack introduced Shelly and Lisa, and Aaron offered to take them all out to see some whales. The three of them were excited. Aaron took them out, and sure enough before long, they found some. All of them were amazed.

"Look at that," said Shelly. "That's so cool!"

All of a sudden, a whale splashed some water onto the boat. They were all shocked.

"Woah!" said Jack.

Shelly couldn't believe it. "That was cool!"

Lisa was drenched. "But we all got wet."

"It's going to be hot," Shelly said. "Our clothes will dry soon."

An hour passed, they were at the ocean and the temperature was rising.

"It's getting hot," said Shelly. "Let's go!"

Lisa got up. "Okay Shelly. Let's go, Jack."

"Fine," Jack said. "Let's go to Lisa's house. I heard it's far."

"Yeah, we go there by bus," said Shelly. "It's about four hours away."

They soon got back to the shore and said their goodbyes to Aaron. He wished them well and invited them to come back any time. They started heading to the bus terminal to catch a bus to Lisa's house.

When they got to the bus terminal, Lisa said "Come on guys, hurry up! The bus is right there, soon it will leave. We don't want to miss the bus. It's going to take another thirty minutes for another bus to come."

They soon hopped on the bus. About four hours later, they got to the town of Hillside, where Lisa's house was. When they got to the city, there was no transportation available. They looked around and started wandering. It was quiet outside, with only a few people walking and a couple vehicles passing by. Lisa tried to call her parents, but nobody answered. She kept trying to call until one of her parents picked up the phone.

Meanwhile, there was a farmer herding his cows from a field nearby onto the dirt road. Some cows were taking a poop along the way. One cow stopped close by where Jack and Shelly were standing; however Jack was facing away and didn't see the cow approach. The farmer whipped the cow, tried to get it going, but the cow just let out a long moo—it was taking a poop.

Jack heard the cow and then turned around. That's when the smell hit him.

"Yuck!"

"That's disgusting!" Shelly said.

The farmer then said, "Sorry about that, these cows are always hard to deal with."

Jack replied, "It's fine, we understand."

Jack and Shelly covered their noses and turned away. Lisa was still busy on the phone. She noticed, but she didn't pay any attention. She was more worried about getting home.

She kept calling for about fifteen minutes, but no one answered the phone.

Just then her next-door neighbor drove up.

"Hey Lisa, do you need a ride?"

"Oh hi, Robert," she said. "Thank God you're passing by. Yes, a ride would be great. These are my friends, Jack and Shelly. Jack, Shelly, this is Robert, my friend who lives next door."

He greeted them warmly and then they piled into his car, and they drove twenty minutes to Lisa's house.

"Thanks, Robert!" said Lisa when they got out.

"Any time," said Robert.

Lisa's mother and father, named Catalina and Morgan, greeted them.

"Mom and dad, I've been trying to call, but nobody answered, where have you guys been?"

"We were just coming home from the garden," Morgan said.

"Yeah," said Catalina, "your father and I were tending vegetables."

"Okay. By the way, these are my friends, Shelly and Jack."

"Hello, come on in," said Catalina.

Lisa then went to her room.

Lisa's house was secluded and far from the city.

"Sorry, our house is so small," Morgan said.

"That's fine," Jack said, "It's nice out here."

"Yeah, I love it," said Shelly. "The area is so clean, serene, no debris, the sound of the water and birds chirping, just love it."

Catalina smiled. "Thank you."

Lisa then came out. "Hi guys come on, I will show you around."

It was almost five, and Catalina was starting to cook dinner. Morgan told them to have fun and that food would be waiting for them when they got back.

Lisa took them to the well.

There was water coming down from the mountain into the well. The well was more like a spring, but it had characteristics like a well and a spring.

"Look at that water," Shelly said. "It's so clean and clear like polished glass."

She ran towards the well. "Is the well shallow or deep?"

"It's shallow," Lisa said. "You can take a bath in it. But be careful, the edge around it is usually slippery."

As Shelly was about to enter the well, she slipped and fell into the water.

"Are you alright?" Lisa asked.

"Yes, I'm fine."

Shelly then started playing in the well. "The water is so *warm*! This is great!"

"I love this!" Jack said, "It's so nice, this is my first time seeing something like this with my very own eyes."

They then all entered the well. The water was over flowing and running into a creek that connected to it.

"Enjoy it, guys," Lisa said. "There is nothing like this in the city."

"You got that right!" Jack said.

Jack was very happy to not be around the hustle and bustle of the city.

"The city is so annoying," Shelly said. "So loud from all the cars, people, machines, along with dirty air and water. We have to buy clean water all the time."

Eventually, Lisa looked around and noticed the time. "Let's go guys, it's already dark. Let's go back in the house, have some dinner, and get some rest."

They all headed to Lisa's house.

As Shelly finished sharing her experience, Jessica said, "Sounds great."

"Yes, it was."

"As you mentioned the well," Jessica said, "I remembered that I got a call from my mother about a mysterious well that appeared in my town. People from all over the place come there."

"Really? I want to see it."

"Well, do you have any plans this weekend?"

"No."

"You can come with me," Jessica said. "I'm going home on Saturday."

"I'd love to. How do we get there?"

"By bus, it's gonna take around two hours. Then, we have to take another small bus going to my neighborhood, which will take about thirty minutes, but we are also going to take local public transportation. So, it's gonna take longer."

Shelly shrugged. "Okay."

Just then Jack came by. "Hey guys."

"What's up Jack?" asked Jessica.

"Not much," he said. "Any plans this weekend?"

"Yeah, do you want to come with us? Shelly and I are gonna visit a mysterious well."

"Where?"

"In my town."

"Oh yeah," he said. "Mysterious huh?"

Shelly smiled. "Yes, very."

"Okay then," he said. "I'm game."

"We will leave on Saturday morning by bus," Jessica said.

"Sure," said Jack. No problem."

2

The Well's Water

On Saturday morning, Jessica, Shelly, and Jack were about to leave the house and head to Jessica's house. Ruby was curious about what they were up to. "Where are you guys going?"

"We're going to my house."

"All of you?" Ruby asked.

"Yeah!" Jessica said.

"Is there something special going on over there?"

Jack smiled. "A mysterious well just appeared over there."

"Yeah," said Shelly. "That's why we're going there. People are coming there from everywhere."

Ruby was amazed. "Is that true, Jessica?"

"Yeah, it's true. My mom just called me yesterday about it. The water is very magical. By the way, the well is actually in a former cemetery. It was found out that the well appeared on the grave of a holy priest that died years ago. There was no well there until recently. There was also no stream of water nearby it, either. Isn't that interesting?"

"Woah," said Jack. "That is amazing!"

Shelly nodded. "That's cool!"

"Wow, that sounds awesome! Can I come?" Ruby asked.

"Sure," Jessica said. "Let's go, get ready. We're waiting right here in the porch."

"Okay." Ruby rushed into her room to pack some clothes.

Before she got to her room, Jessica called out. "We are going to stay at my house overnight."

"Okay," she called back. "I will make sure to bring enough clothes."

"You don't have to. I have plenty of clothes at home. You can wear mine."

"It's fine," Ruby said. "These aren't heavy anyway. Thank you though. Just wait until I get ready."

"Alright." Jessica said.

They were all ready and started walking towards a bus stop. They left at nine o'clock in the morning. It took ten minutes to walk there. They had to cross the street three times.

"Come on, guys," Jessica said. "The bus is going to arrive in five minutes!"

"Wait up guys!" said Shelly who was lagging behind.

"Come on, Shelly. Hurry up!"

A couple minutes later, as soon as they crossed the street for a second time, Jessica saw a bus coming.

"Quickly, the bus is arriving!"

They started running.

"We can't run across the street with all this traffic," said Jack. "We'll have to wait for the next bus."

Without notice, the light turned red.

"There," said Jessica. "Let's run quickly!"

The bus stopped, and they all hopped on.

Jessica then noticed some empty seats at the front of the bus.

"Let's sit over at the front, so we can get a good view of the outside." said Jessica.

Then they all sat down and waited until they got to their destination.

Two hours later, they arrived at the large city of Newtown, where Jessica's family lived. When they got off the bus, there were many people selling empty gallon jugs.

Ruby was surprised. "There's so many people here! Is everybody going to the well?"

"Probably most of them," Jessica said.

"I don't understand," Shelly said. "Why are there people selling empty jugs?"

"It's because of the well," Jessica said. "People buy jugs to bring water from the well back to their homes."

Jack, Ruby, and Shelly each bought a jug. Jessica did not, since her parents lived nearby the well.

"Okay Jessica," said Jack, "where are we going now?"

"We're going to take a minibus to get to my neighborhood."

A local minibus was already there, waiting for people to get on. The transportation in the area was mostly not run or controlled by the local government. Public transport was usually privately ran, which meant the buses didn't follow a strict schedule. The drivers usually just left whenever the bus was full. They all piled on the bus. Some of the people on the bus were going home from the farms, the markets, and the city itself. Others were just visitors. A few people brought their pets, others brought groceries from nearby stores, and others still brought vegetables and fruit from a nearby farmer's market. The bus was packed. Jack was sitting beside a man who had a puppy on his right. The puppy tried to lick Jack's face. Jack jerked away. The puppy's owner saw this and stopped the puppy. On the other side of the man, however, was Shelly. After the puppy stopped messing with Jack, it sat back on its owner's lap and started wagging its tail. Its tail, however, was whacking Shelly. The man didn't notice, and so he didn't do anything.

About an hour later, they arrived at Jessica's town, a place called Green Mountain, where the well was located. They all got off the minibus.

"That puppy on the bus kept whacking me with its tail." Shelly said. "I wanted to say something, but there were people around, and I didn't want to make a scene."

"Well, look at my sandals!" Ruby said. "Somebody stepped on them and now there's mud all over them!"

"And the same puppy tried to lick me," Jack said. "I had to move out of the way!"

"Sorry, guys, for the trouble," Jessica said. "We still have to walk for fifteen minutes to my house."

They all started walking towards Jessica's house.

When they finally arrived, Jessica opened the door, it wasn't locked. Her parents, however, knew that she was coming. The house was empty, as they were still at the farm. The house was huge. It had four bedrooms, one big kitchen, two bathrooms, and a giant living room. Nevertheless, it was only one floor. The house and floor were made out of brick.

"Welcome guys to my house!" Jessica said. "I'll show you your rooms. You can get cleaned up, and then get some rest."

"Where's the bathroom?" Shelly said. "I want to clean up my shoes."

"Me too!" Ruby said.

"I'll show you, it's over here."

Jessica walked them to the bathroom. Ten minutes later, Jessica's parents arrived home. Jessica heard them coming and came out of her room.

"Hey Mom and Dad! I brought some friends here."

Jack, Shelly, and Ruby heard them and came out their rooms. Ruby and Shelly shared a room, and Jack was in a room by himself. He introduced himself.

"Hello, my name is Jack."

Jessica's mom smiled at him. "Oh hi! My name is Emma. Welcome to our house, I hope you get comfortable!"

"Hi, I'm Shelly! This is my friend, Ruby! She's the daughter of the owner of the house we live in."

"Jack is Ruby's nephew," Jessica added.

"Oh, welcome all," said Jessica's dad. "I'm Matthew. It's nice to meet you. Make yourself at home."

"You guys must be hungry," Emma said. "It's almost one!"

"Yeah," said Jessica. "We just went straight here."

"I'm going to cook some lunch," Emma said. "You guys just get some rest."

"Can I help in the kitchen?" Ruby asked.

"No, it's alright! Just relax."

"Come on guys," Jessica said. "Let me show you around!"

Jessica then showed them to the backyard, where there were fruits and vegetables planted around. She also brought a small basket. About one hour later, Jessica's mom called for them.

"Come on guys! Food is ready!"

They all entered the house and walked to the kitchen.

"Hey," said Jessica, "I'll show you guys the well tomorrow. It's been quite a trip, so let's just relax for today."

"Sounds good to me," said Jack.

Ruby nodded. "Okay, I can't wait to see the well!"

"Yeah," said Shelly. "I bet it's going to be cool!"

Later that evening, they were in the dining room. They already finished dinner and were talking about the well.

"Hey, Mom," said Jessica. "What can you tell is about the well, since we're going there tomorrow?"

Emma thought for a moment. "Well, there was this couple, Walter and Mackenzie Goff, who brought their little girl over to the water. Now, this is a bit funny, because the parents wanted to stop her from constantly being fussy or crying. Their daughter, a pretty two-year-old girl named Stephanie, was always crying about something. It didn't matter what it was, she would cry over it. One day, Walter had an idea to take her down to the well.

"So, they brought her to the well and had her take a bath in the water. Abruptly, she stopped crying. They went back home, happy that their daughter had stopped crying. However, hours later, they had noticed that their daughter didn't say anything or even react with any emotion. They both noticed this weird quirk and decided that the well had something to do with it, so they took her back. After they took her back to the water, the daughter started crying again as she normally did."

After listening to the story, Ruby looked to the others. "Wow, that's so weird!"

Jack nodded. "Definitely not something you hear every day."

"You got that right!" said Shelly.

"Wow, Mom, that's unreal! It's just so unimaginable."

But Emma wasn't done.

"There was a different couple, Henry and Scarlett Livingston, who wanted to cheer up their son. He was always sad and never wanted to do anything, not even eat. Tyler, the son, had recently broken up with his girlfriend. After Henry and Scarlett heard about the mysterious, magical well nearby, they discussed if they should bring Tyler there.

"After some discussion, they did just that. After bathing in the water for a couple minutes and drinking some of the water, Tyler started smiling. He seemed happy, and so the parents were very excited. They came back home. Tyler was still smiling. Scarlett noticed that, but she assumed that he was just very happy. A couple hours later, his mother noticed that he was still smiling.

"Scarlett then scolded him and told him to help his father. So Tyler went out and saw his father washing the car. Henry then told Tyler to help him.

"And still, Tyler was smiling. Henry assumed he was just happy. A few minutes later, his father slipped on the floor. He saw that Tyler was still smiling, even laughing at him. That's when Henry knew that there was something wrong.

"He quickly went into the house and talked to his wife. They both decided that something was wrong, as this behavior was definitely weird and not right.

"They soon took him back to the well and after a couple of minutes, he returned to being sad again. However, his father and mother decided to just let him go through it."

"That's hilarious!" Jack said. "It's also very strange."

"That's so odd and a little creepy," Shelly said.

"I know," Emma said. "Well, you guys should get ready to go to sleep and get some rest for tomorrow."

"Okay, Mom," Jessica said.

Everybody then got ready to go to sleep. A few hours later, they were all asleep.

Next morning, after they finished breakfast, everybody started packing their bags. They were planning to go home, after they visited the well.

"Hey guys," Jessica said. "Get ready quickly so that we have time to check out the well for a bit! We don't want to go home too late."

"Alright, well I'm already ready," Jack said.

"Okay," said Ruby. "I'm almost ready to go."

Shelly was flustered. "Give me five minutes, I will be ready!"

Before they left, Jessica called for her parents.

"Mom, Dad! My friends and I are going to the well! We're going to go to the city after that."

"Alright," Matthew called back. "Be careful out there!"

Emma came into the room and gave Jessica a hug. "Okay sweetie, take care!"

"We will, Mom!"

They left the house at around nine in the morning. Jack, Shelly, and Ruby brought their gallon jugs to fill up with the water from the well. The well was around fifteen minutes away from the house when on foot. On their way to the well, there were still several people selling empty gallon jugs. The neighborhood was large, but it had sparsely populated areas. Every house had more than moderately-sized backyards and gardens. Most of the people who lived there were working in farms and gardens. However, others worked in the nearby cities. The well was close to the mountains, in the foothills.

When they got to the well, there were many news teams at the area reporting on the event. They also saw something else. The well was being blocked by some pipes, and they couldn't see the well entirely. The well itself was loosely in the shape of a man-made well; however, it was more like a type of spring. There was water coming down from the mountain, which used to fall into the well. After the installation of the pipes, the stream was redirected into a pool. People used the pipes from the well to collect water, while people used the pool for bathing. There was also water coming up from underneath into the well.

Shelly looked confused.

"Why are there so many pipes?"

"They're here so that the people can easily get access to the water. It's to make sure people don't hoard the water or wait in long lines."

"I guess that makes sense," said Jack

Everybody who was there were either bathing in the water or collecting the water. However, Jack, Shelly, and Ruby decided to just wash their faces and each get a gallon of the water to bring home. Jessica, however, only washed her face, since she did not bring a gallon jug. While Jessica was waiting for her friends, she turned to her right and saw somebody carrying someone who couldn't walk. When the man was bathed in the water, he could suddenly walk again. Shelly saw somebody who was blind go to the water, with the help of somebody else.

Shelly turned to Jack and nudged him in the side. "Pssst, Jack, look."

After bathing in the water, the person was able to see. Then Ruby saw a woman walking to the water. It appeared that she couldn't talk. When she bathed into the water, she was then able to talk again. Others, who were fine, drank the water in hope of having the water keep them healthy or even attractive. After they all got their gallons of water, they decided it was time to go home.

"Hey guys," Jessica said. "Let's start heading back to the bus stop and go home."

"Okay, I'm fine with that," said Shelly.

Around twenty minutes later, they reached a bus and rode back to the city.

3

A Ghostly Visitor

After Shelly got back home to Scarcetree, she was wondering if she should go home to bring the gallon of water to Dogwood to help people over there who couldn't go to the well. Next Saturday, she finally decided to go home and visit her parents.

Nine o'clock, on Saturday morning, she packed her bags, brought the gallon jug, and got ready to leave.

Before she left, Shelly found Ruby in the kitchen washing dishes.

"Hey Ruby, I'm going to go to my parents' house. I'll be back tomorrow."

"Oh, I thought you were going home in a couple of weeks."

"I was," said Shelly, "but I have decided to go home today instead, so I can bring this gallon of water. Do you know where Lisa and Jessica are?"

"They already left to go to get something to eat."

"Okay, tell them I had to go visit my parents and that I'll see them tomorrow."

"Alright," said Ruby, drying her hands. "Take care."

Shelly exited the house and started heading to the bus stop.

Ten minutes later, the bus arrived. Shelly hopped on. Three hours later, she arrived at Dogwood. Before she got off the bus, she called her brother.

"Hey Tony, I'm in Dogwood. I'm going to visit mom and dad. Will you pick me up?"

Tony sounded surprised. *"You came home early? What's going on?"*

"Oh, nothing," she said. "I just wanted to visit home."

"Oh, okay. Give me fifteen minutes, I'll be there."

"Alright. Thanks."

Five minutes later, Shelly got off the bus. She started to wait for her brother to arrive. Tony was five years older than Shelly. He worked and lived in the city, while his parents lived nearby the city. Around ten minutes later, her brother arrived.

"Hey Shelly! Get in!"

Shelly got in the car, and they started driving home.

"What you got there?" Tony asked.

"It's a gallon of water."

"Why're you bringing a gallon of water? There's plenty of water at home."

"It is water from the magical well at Green Mountain, where my friend Jessica lives."

"Really?"

"Yeah."

"Hmm, interesting."

Soon, they arrived. Shelly saw her father, Harrison, out in the living room at the front of the house. She went and threw open the door and ran over to him.

"Hey Dad!"

Harrison's eyes widened. "Oh my, look who's come home early!"

Shelly put down the jug of water and gave him a hug. He called over his shoulder.

"Hey honey, Shelly's home."

A moment later, Casey, her mom, came out from the kitchen while rubbing her hands on her apron.

"This is terrific, what a wonderful surprise," she said hugging her daughter.

"Hi Mom, what were you doing?"

"I was cooking. Oh, it's a good thing you're here, since the food is almost ready. I bet you're hungry!"

"I'm starving!"

"So, how was the trip?" Harrison asked.

"Oh, it was good. Tony picked me up."

"Yes, I see that. He could have told us he was picking you up, but that was good of him." He looked down at his daughter's feet. "Why did you bring a water jug? We have water here."

"This is special water, Dad. It's from a sacred well."

Harrison narrowed his eyes. "Oh really? Well, give it to your mother. She can put it away."

Shelly picked up the jug and handed it to her mom.

"What did you say this was again, Shelly?"

"It's magical water from a sacred well. It can cure the incurable. I've seen it with my own eyes."

"Are you sure?" Casey sounded skeptical.

"I'm positive, Mom. That's why I brought an entire gallon."

"Alright, I'll put it away when we enter the house. Where's Tony?"

"He's outside by the car."

Casey went out the house and called for her son. "Hey Tony! Come over here and join us for lunch! Lunch is almost ready!"

"Alright," he said. "Coming!"

Soon, they all got ready for lunch. Before entering the kitchen, Shelly went into her room with her bags.

Her mother said, "I cleaned your room."

"I see, thanks Mom."

Shelly changed her clothes and went to the dining room. Casey placed the gallon of well water by her bed. Then she entered the dining room. They all had lunch together.

After finishing lunch, Tony had to get to work, but he promised Shelly he'd stop by and see her tomorrow.

Later in the afternoon, at around five, Shelly just got out from her room, after taking a rest. She saw her mother carrying a bucket.

"What is in that bucket, Mom?"

"Fish."

"Are we having fish for dinner?"

"Yeah, I'm going to cut it up."

"Are you going to fry or bake?"

"Your father wants it baked."

Shelly smiled. "Oh, I love baked fish!"

"I know," Casey said. "That's why your father wanted baked. He knows you love it."

"Can I help you make dinner?" Shelly asked.

"You can help cut the vegetables. I'll cut the fish."

"Okay."

Soon, Shelly and Casey went to the kitchen. Shelly was getting vegetables from the refrigerator and started cutting them up with a board and knife. Her mother started cutting the fish. All of a sudden, her mother yelped.

"What's wrong? What happened?!"

"I cut my finger!"

"Are you alright Mom, do you need to go to the doctor?"

"No," Casey said quickly, "No, I will be fine."

"You should try the magical well water, it could probably heal you."

Casey sounded reluctant. "Oh, I don't need it. I just need some sort of bandage, and it will be fine."

She started wrapping her finger with some cloth. They continued cutting up the food and started cooking. Around an hour later, the food was ready.

"Where's your father? Call for him and tell him dinner is ready."

Shelly came out to find her father. Harrison was fixing the gutter.

"Dad, dinner is ready! Come on!"

Harrison stopped working on the gutter. "Okay, coming in a second."

A couple minutes later, they were all in the dining room. Harrison looked over at Casey.

"What happened to your finger?" He sounded quite concerned.

"Oh, I was just cutting fish, and I cut my finger."

"Do you need to go to the doctor?"

"No, no, I will be fine."

"Are you sure? We can go right now."

"It's fine," she said firmly. "I don't need to go to the doctor."

A few minutes later, after they were done with dinner, they watched TV together.

Shelly then asked, "How is grandma doing?"

"She's doing fine," said Harrison.

"Shelly, are you going to visit your grandma tomorrow?" Casey asked.

"I don't think I can, since I'm going to leave tomorrow. I will need rest when I get home, so I'm just going to call her instead. When you see her, just tell her that I didn't have enough time to come and visit."

Casey replied, "Alright then."

A few hours later, they were all getting sleepy.

"I'm tired," Shelly said. "I'm going to get some sleep."

"Okay honey," Casey said. "Get some rest. Have a good night."

"Okay, thanks Mom. Good night, guys."

Harrison turned to her and gave her a nod. "Good night, honey."

Shelly went to her room, turned off the lights, and went straight to bed.

In bed, Casey was worried and couldn't sleep. Her finger was throbbing, but she didn't want to go to the hospital because she didn't have any insurance. She didn't want to pay a lot of money on medical care because Shelly's schooling required a lot of money. Shelly was going to an expensive, major private school.

Once Harrison fell asleep, Casey started to cry because the pain was getting worse, and she couldn't drift off. She didn't want to wake up everybody, either. She then remembered the water, but she didn't want to use it, since she didn't think it would work. She had never heard of the special powers of the well water, only hearing it from Shelly. At midnight, while she was crying, a very old man in white robes with a long, white beard appeared in front of her in the room. His voice was calm.

"Casey, drink some of the water from the gallon and pour some on your finger."

He then unexpectedly disappeared in a flash. Casey both in surprise and in a hurry, picked up the gallon nearby her bed, and she opened it. She did what the mysterious old man told her, and immediately her finger stopped having pain. It was also cured. Then she went back to bed and slept soundly until morning.

Next morning, Casey was already in the kitchen making breakfast. Shelly came to the kitchen.

"Hey Mom, good morning."

"Good morning, sweetie. How was your sleep?"

"Oh, it was great! How is your finger?"

Casey put down the spatula she was holding and turned to her daughter. "Oh honey, I couldn't sleep last night. The pain was very great. I started crying, then all of a sudden, an old man appeared and told me to drink the water from the gallon jug then pour some of it on my finger. As soon as I did, the pain went away, and my finger went back to normal."

Shelly was shocked. "Woah! The old man must be the holy priest that died a long time ago! Mom, the well appeared on a cemetery, and it was on the priest's grave."

Casey understood. "Oh, he must have visited me. I guess he likes helping people."

"Yeah," said Shelly, "that's what I heard he did when he was still alive. He helped lots of people." Shelly looked around. "Where's dad?"

"I'm not sure. He might be still fixing the gutter outside."

A minute later, Harrison called from outside. "Casey! Tony is here!"

Shelly went out to meet him.

"Oh, hey Tony! It's a good thing you're here! You're going to take me to the bus station, right?"

"Of course, when are you going to leave?"

"After lunch."

Then, Casey came out. "Oh, I'm so happy you came to help your sister get to the bus station!"

"Sure," Tony said, "I'm glad to be able to help my sister."

They all walked back into the house.

"Well your timing is good," Casey said, "Did you have breakfast? You can eat with us. Come on."

"Great," Tony said. "What's for breakfast?"

"Scrambled eggs, sausage, bacon, and toast."

"Oh, sounds great!"

Harrison clapped his son on the back. "Come on Tony, sit down and eat with us!"

"Alright."

As they ate, Harrison asked, "Hey Tony, tell us a bit about your job. How is it going?"

"Yeah Tony," Shelly said. "I want to know!"

"The job is in a hotel. I'm a front desk clerk. It's going well."

"Oh great!" Casey said. "I'm glad to hear that."

"That's good, Son," said Harrison.

Tony turned to Shelly. "How is your school?"

"It's good."

"That's great to hear," Tony said.

A few hours later, in the afternoon, Shelly got ready to leave. She packed her bags and exited the house. Her brother and parents were outside, waiting for her.

"Ready to go, honey?" Casey asked.

"Yes, Mom." Shelly gave her a hug. "Bye Mom, I love you."

"I love you, too. Take care and stay safe."

"I will, don't worry."

"Get home safe and take care of yourself," Harrison said. Shelly also gave him a hug. "Okay Dad, I love you."

"I love you, too."

Tony went to the car. "Bye Mom and Dad, I'll see you next weekend! Come on, Shelly."

Harrison and Casey stood there waving as they pulled away and Tony headed for the bus station.

4
Taking Advantage

About a year later in early summer of 2006, when Shelly had just come back from school in her home in Scarcetree on a Friday afternoon, she entered her room, dropped her backpack, and changed into her house clothes. She went to find Jessica to see if she wanted to get some food. She knocked on Jessica's room door.

"Jessica, are you there?"

"Yeah, I'm here."

She opened the door and came out.

"Hey, what are you doing right now?"

"Oh, I'm just relaxing on the bed."

"You wanna go out and get some food?"

"Oh sure! Give a second, I need to get my money."

A few minutes later, they left on foot to a nearby supermarket.

Thirty minutes later, they were on their way back home with some food. They started talking about what they should do on the weekend.

"So what are you planning for the weekend?" asked Shelly.

Jessica shrugged. "I'm planning to go home."

"What about your boyfriend?"

"He's not going to come with me this time," she said. "He's going to stay here. Besides, I'm going to leave early morning tomorrow and come back in the late afternoon. What about you, what are you going to do tomorrow?"

"Nothing, really."

"Wanna come?"

Shelly brightened. "Sure! It sounds fun. Can we visit the mysterious well, too?"

"Absolutely!"

Eventually, they reached home where they entered their rooms and brought the food with them.

Next morning, they got up and started preparing to leave. Around two hours later, they reached Newtown. Unlike before, there wasn't anybody selling jugs for the well. There weren't that many people heading to the neighborhood, either. When Shelly looked out the window, she was befuddled due to the low amount of people in the area, compared to before. Before they got off the bus, Jessica called her parents.

"Dad, I'm arriving at the bus stop in Newtown. Will you pick me up? I'm also with one of my friends."

"Of course, wait there. It's going to take a while, so find a place nearby to maybe eat or just rest."

"Okay, Dad."

After she disconnected the call, Jessica turned to Shelly. "Let's get something to eat, I'm hungry. You're hungry, aren't you?"

"Yeah, I'm famished!"

"My father's gonna pick us up," Jessica said. "But it's gonna take a while, because he's far away. I should have called him earlier."

"That's okay," Shelly said, pointing to a small restaurant at the corner of the intersection. "We can wait in that small restaurant right there."

"Okay," said Jessica. "Let's go there."

Around thirty minutes later, Matthew arrived. Jessica saw his car and flagged him down. He greeted them both warmly and took them to Jessica's house.

About half hour later, they pulled up and everybody got out of the car and entered the house.

Jessica called out a couple of times for her mom.

"She's probably in the backyard," Matthew said. "Shelly, why don't you take a seat and make yourself at home."

"Thank you."

Shelly sat down. Jessica ran to the backyard, looking for her mother. She saw her mother picking up fruits and vegetables.

"Hey Mom!"

Emma looked up then turned around.

"Hey, you're already here! Are you hungry?"

"No, I just ate with Shelly while waiting for Dad to pick us up."

"Oh, you brought Shelly? Where is she?"

"She's waiting in the living room. Come on, let's see her."

"You left her there by herself?"

"No, Dad's with her."

Jessica and her mother then headed to the living room.

Emma saw their guest. "Hi Shelly, welcome back to our house."

"Thank you, you guys are so kind. Sorry to trouble you."

"Come on, Shelly," Jessica said. "You're like our family, right Mom and Dad?"

Emma smiled. "We're happy to have you, Shelly."

"No trouble at all," Matthew said.

Shelly felt very cherished. "Thank you."

"I'll go up and make up a room," said Emma.

"No, that's okay, Mom," Jessica said. "We aren't gonna stay overnight."

Emma looked a little crestfallen. "Why not?"

"I have plans tomorrow with Ronny," Jessica said. "We're gonna visit his parents' house."

"Oh yeah, your boyfriend!" Matthew said. "Why is he not with you?"

"He's busy today." Jessica said. "Anyway, Shelly wants to go to the well, I'm going to take her there."

"When? Right now?" Emma asked.

"Yeah, we don't want to be too late."

"Aren't you guys tired," Matthew said. "Don't you want to rest?"

"No, we're fine, Dad."

"Do you want me to take you there?"

Jessica turned to Shelly. "What do you think?"

"Nah," she said. "Let's just walk there, it's more refreshing, if that's okay with you."

"That's fine with me," Jessica said.

"Alright then," he said. "Don't be out too long. Come home for lunch."

"Yes," Emma said, "I'm going to cook lunch, it's going to be ready when you guys come back home."

"Okay. Thanks, Mom. Let's go, Shelly!"

Fifteen minutes later, they arrived at the well. Unlike a year ago, along the street to the well, there were many businesses and booths nearby. Not many people, however, were selling jugs. Instead, businesses were selling products related to the well for people walking by. When they got to the well, there were few people there. However, there were still a few news reporters and news vans nearby reporting about the well.

Shelly looked around. "Why aren't there as many people here as before?"

Jessica shrugged. "People use this area for business and commerce. Apparently, the well water is less effective."

"Oh," said Shelly, thinking about the old man who'd appeared to her mother. "I guess that makes sense."

Over time, businessmen nearby noticed that the well water was no longer as effective as before. They decided that they were not supposed to make business off of it. For a while, not many people came, thinking the well would never return to its previous effectiveness.

However, the well still stands.

The few that still come believe that it is still very special. Some simply believe the well is less effective due to the businesses and unnecessary usage of the well. But others believe that if you pray and believe in things holy, the well still works and does still cure the incurable. Those people who still believe in the power of the well say that it simply no longer serves *everybody*—and instead serves the people who pray, believe, and are pure.

BIZARRE REPTILES

I

Released & Returned

Once upon a time in the early summer of 2002, a twenty-five-year-old woman named Maya worked and lived in a city named Victorious. Victorious was a massive, metropolitan city. It had many luxurious buildings and hotels in the downtown area. She lived nearby a central business district. All kinds of businesses were there, you could find almost anything: supermarkets, hotels, banks, restaurants, department stores, almost everything. She could even go to these places on foot.

In the outskirts of the city, there was a large, busy international airport. There were major international businesses located in the area. It only took a few minutes to walk to these places. She lived in a two-story house with three rooms downstairs, four rooms upstairs. The house also had two living rooms and two bathrooms, both upstairs and downstairs. There was also a kitchen downstairs. Maya had seven roommates, but her closest roommate was Maggie.

Maya and all her roommates were working. Some were working in restaurants; some were in department stores. Maya was feisty, outgoing, and independent. Her hair was short, above the shoulders, and curly. Maya worked as a tour guide at a travel agency and studied in college. Maggie was thirty-two years old, and she lived next to her room upstairs. She worked at a government office. Maggie was laid-back, yet outgoing. She didn't speak a lot, and she smoked cigarettes. She liked to listen to stories and also jokes.

One Saturday afternoon, Maya and her roommate Maggie were sitting on a couch in the living room. Maya was eating noodles for breakfast, which she ordered from a restaurant nearby, and her roommate was reading a newspaper.

"Hey Maggie, what's the headline on the newspaper? I can't quite make it out."

"It's about a woman giving birth to a baby alligator."

"What, how is that possible? Is there a picture of it? Let me see."

Maggie nodded. "Yeah, it's right here."

She pointed to the picture. It was a picture of an alligator lying down on a luxurious bed in a house.

Maya shook her head. "Wow, that's weird, but amazing. Can you read from the beginning on what happened?"

"Okay, so it started off with the lady in a new couple getting pregnant. This couple lives in a small town, far from here and any major city. There were no hospitals close in the area, either…"

In a small town called Green Valley, a young wife named Patricia, was lying down in bed.

All of a sudden, she called out for her husband. "Roger, I think my water broke!"

Roger sat up quickly. "Okay, let's go to the hospital. I'll call a cab."

"We can't," Patricia shouted. "It's about to come out!"

Roger was frantic. "Really, that fast?!"

"I don't know, it feels like it!"

Half an hour later, the baby was born. Roger was shocked to find out that his baby was not a human baby at all. Instead, it was an alligator.

Patricia was also surprised and shocked. "What? How is that possible?!"

As they were looking at the alligator, both of them felt sad and confused. Then, they started talking about it. They finally had a decision. They decided to put the baby alligator in the river. A couple minutes later, Roger headed towards the nearby river. Then, he gently placed the baby alligator in the river. The baby alligator, however, stayed there. He walked away, sad and disappointed.

About a month later, the baby alligator was much bigger. However, he stayed in the same area where he'd been left. Anytime he saw children in the river, he just looked at them and never approached them. One day, the young alligator decided to approach a group of young kids, around five to seven years old, playing in the river. However, the kids got scared and all of them quickly jumped out of the river.

"Watch out," one kid had screamed. "There's an alligator! Get out of the river!"

All the kids soon left the river. The young alligator swam back and stayed at the riverbank.

Later that night, Patricia had a dream. In the dream, the alligator was calling for her.

"Mother, mother, I'm your son."

Patricia soon woke up and told her husband about it.

"I had an odd dream that the alligator called me and said that it was my son!"

Next morning, they went back to the river, looking for the alligator. They found the alligator at the same area, on the riverbank. When the alligator saw the couple, he got out of the water. Roger picked him up, and Patricia started crying. They soon brought him home. Some nearby people saw this and started visiting the couple. The parents were poor. Since people were visiting them frequently, the couple decided to charge money for people to see him. That way, they could afford to raise the alligator. When there was nobody around and the alligator was hungry, he usually went to the kitchen to help himself with something to eat. Some reporters soon visited the couple and interviewed them about the alligator.

After Maggie finished reading the newspaper story, Maya almost didn't know what to say.

"Wow, that's so weird, yet amazing!"

"It is definitely very strange," said Maggie, "and also so sad. It is unfortunate that the alligator was just left in the river."

Then, they heard someone going upstairs. Maya turned around, and saw it was her twenty-two-year-old brother, Arnold. Arnold was energetic and friendly and had short, black hair. Arnold worked at a garment factory. He also lived fifteen miles away from Maya's place, near an airport.

"Oh, hey Arnold! I thought you went to visit Mom and Dad."

"Yeah," he said. "I just got back yesterday."

"How are you doing, Arnold?" Maggie asked.

"Good, how are you?"

"I'm good," Maggie said. "Come sit down here with us."

"Alright."

Maggie then picked up a cigarette from a cigarette box and offered it to Arnold.

"Want a cigarette?"

WOMAN GIVES BIRTH
TO ALLIGATOR

"No thanks," he said. "I don't smoke. Since when did *you* start smoking?"

Maggie shrugged. "Only recently."

Maya turned to him. "How are Mom and Dad doing?"

"They are doing great."

"I'm glad to hear that."

Arnold saw the newspaper with the headline WOMAN GIVES BIRTH TO ALLIGATOR. He then picked it up.

"Whose newspaper is this?"

"Maggie's," Maya said.

"You know," said Arnold. "I just heard people on a bus talking about a woman who gave birth to an alligator, but I didn't know that it was in the newspaper."

"It's a weird story," Maggie said.

"I know," he said. "I heard another weird story, too, which I heard yesterday. It's a weird story about a crocodile, not an alligator."

Maggie sat up straight, clearly curious. "Can you tell us about it?"

And so he did.

2

The Fisherman &
The Crocodile

"Maya," he said, "you know where people have to cross the Stamtona River by ferry because they can't build a bridge?"

"I know what you are talking about. Next to our town, we cross the river by ferry anytime we go to the city. That is because it's faster than going around and crossing a bridge in a different town, which takes about an hour. It's half an hour shorter."

"Do you know *why* they can't build a bridge?"

Maya nodded. "Of course, according to a local legend, the river is home to a mysterious crocodile. The mysterious crocodile would not allow people to build a bridge. They can only build a bridge when they're willing to sacrifice an entire family."

"What?" Maggie said, "That's weird and creepy. What happens if people build a bridge anyway?"

"Who knows," Maya said. "They say if people were to build a bridge anyway, a disaster would happen. The bridge could collapse and never stay standing or people could die."

Arnold nodded. "That's why they don't build a bridge."

"I thought they were just superstitious people," Maya said. "However, I remember on a ferry crossing the river, I heard someone telling a story about the crocodile to everybody in the ferry. According to the story, a guy was trying to cross the river in the late evening, when the ferry crossing the river was not running at that time. Then, he saw something. He thought it was a big log flowing across the river, a few feet away from the pier. He used the log to try and cross the river. When he got to the middle of the river, he realized it wasn't a log, and it was in fact a big crocodile. He kept crossing the river until he got to the other side. After he crossed, the crocodile disappeared. He realized that the crocodile was helping him cross the river. I heard that the next day, a group of hunters and fishermen went to the river to hunt the crocodile and kill it. However, after hours of searching in and around the river, they couldn't find it. It's a weird story, do you think it's true?"

"I think so," Arnold said. "What do you think Maggie?"

"It's probably true."

"I think they should still try to build a bridge," Maya said. "How do they know if they never try?"

Arnold shook his head. "They don't want to take a risk. Anyway, yesterday when I got to the river, the ferry was on the other side of the river."

"How did you get there?" Maya said.

"Benny. You know Benny, right?" Arnold asked.

"Yeah, next door neighbor, is he at his house now?"

Arnold nodded. "Yeah, he's been at his house for around a month. After he took me to the river bank, Benny went back home."

"Okay," said Maya, "then what happened?"

Arnold answered, "There was a fisherman, sitting under a tree and waiting for his fishing trap to be ready to be pulled out of the water. So I approached him, because he smiled at me anytime he saw me."

About nine o'clock in the morning, Arnold approached a fisherman and they struck up a conversation and introduced themselves.

The fisherman's name was Joe, a fairly skinny man in his mid-forties. He was a relaxed, friendly, and hard-working individual who had been fishing for many years as both a job and a hobby.

After a while, Arnold gestured towards the trap. "Having much luck?"

Joe replied, "I'm doing well. I'm not doing too badly for trapping, I've seen a few fish here and there. However, it definitely wasn't as good as two nights ago."

"Yeah?" Arnold asked, "what happened two nights ago?"

"Well, I met this very interesting guy in the evening."

Joe was sitting on the bank of the Stamtona that night, waiting until his fishing trap was ready to be checked on. In the late evening, a handsome, young man in clean, casual clothes approached him randomly.

"Hey, can you watch my spare clothes? I'm going to the nightclub nearby."

"Okay, sure," Joe said. "I'll watch them."

"Thanks, friend."

The man soon ran off to the nightclub. At the nightclub, the man danced with different women. Since he was so handsome, all the women wanted to dance with him. Some fought over him, but he ignored them and continued dancing with others instead. Other women tried to ask him to dance with them, offering drinks and other items.

"Hey, dance with me! I'll give you a glass of wine."

"No, dance with me! I'll buy you a can of beer!"

This continued for some time, with some others involved, too. However, the man kept dancing and continued walking away to avoid them and avoid the chaos that sometimes ensued. Eventually, some of the bartenders called for security and the bouncers involved in the party to break up the fighting.

As a result, a few women eventually got kicked out of the nightclub. Some of the other men, who were drunk, in the nightclub got jealous and tried to fight him, too. In spite of that, he simply pushed them away and didn't get involved. The bouncers also grabbed some of the men trying to start fights and threw them out.

A couple hours later, the party ended. The man walked away and went to Joe to get his clothes.

"Thank you for watching my clothes."

"No problem," Joe said.

Then, the man walked a few feet away and changed his clothes. Joe was looking at his trap while the man did so. When Joe turned back to the man, he saw a crocodile, which proceeded to jump into the river. Joe was shocked and a bit scared. He was about to run away with the trap. However, when he pulled the trap, he noticed that the trap was abruptly full of fish. Joe was surprised, since the trap was almost empty when he last checked on it.

For the rest of that night, whenever he threw his trap back into the water, he could check a few minutes later and the trap would be full. He did this until dawn. He gained a lot of fish due to this, and he soon brought it back to his wife at his house, so she could sell it at the nearby market.

Later that evening, Joe went to the nightclub, where the mysterious handsome man went. During that time, there were only a few people in the club. Some were playing pool, and others were at tables. Joe knew the bartender, and always went there when he wanted to get a drink. The bartender was picking up empty glasses and cleaning the table.

The bartender greeted Joe when he saw him.

"Hey Joe, how are you? It's good seeing you, again."

"Oh hey, I'm doing great. How about you?"

"That's great to hear, I'm also doing fine. You want the usual, correct?"

"Yes."

The bartender poured him a drink. "How did your fishing go?"

"It went great, I caught a lot of fish. How was the party last night?"

"There was a lot more chaos than normal; however, it was taken care of. There was this good-looking, young man I had never seen before. He seemed nice, but others wanted to try and get his attention. It was a bit odd."

"Last evening, I also met a handsome man."

"Was he tall with short hair, wearing blue jeans and a black button-up shirt?"

"Exactly! As a matter of fact, he told me to watch his other clothes so he could come here. When he got back, he put his clothes on and jumped in the river! But he wasn't human. I think it was probably that mysterious crocodile that lives in the river. I was scared, but then I realized he gave me a bunch of fish."

"Wow, the mysterious crocodile! I have heard that if you burn his clothes, he can't turn back into a crocodile."

"Really? Did something like that happen before?"

"Not exactly, only something similar. It happened to a snake, not a crocodile. It also happened in a different town."

"Oh, that's interesting. I didn't know those were crocodile clothes. Well, tell me more about it some other time, since I have to go. My wife is probably looking for me, since I didn't tell her I was coming here."

After speaking to the bartender, Joe finished his drink, said his goodbyes, and went out.

After Joe shared his story, Arnold could barely believe it. "Wow, do you think the mysterious crocodile gave you fish?"

Joe nodded. "I believe so."

"So, the mysterious crocodile that lives in the Stamtona River can be nice," said Arnold, "at least it appears so, as long as no one bothers him in this river."

Arnold soon looked at the river and saw that the ferry was already there. People started to get on the ferry.

"Goodbye, Joe! Thank you for sharing that cool story! Good luck fishing!"

"Thank you, it was nice talking to you as well, Arnold."

Arnold picked up his bags and got on the ferry. The ferry soon left.

"That's a very cool story!" Maggie said.

"So strange!" said Maya.

"Yeah," said Arnold. "It is very strange."

Maggie turned to Maya. "Hey, do you have any plans today?"

"Not really," Maya said.

"Want to go to the supermarket and have some lunch outside?"

"Sure, but I have to take a bath first."

"Yeah, me too," Maggie said. "Hey Arnold, want to come?"

"To the market?" Arnold said. "Sure, I'll wait for you guys right here in the living room"

"Have you eaten yet?" Maya asked.

"Nah, I'll eat later when we go to the supermarket. There is a restaurant nearby, we can all eat together."

"Okay," Maya said, "I won't take long."

Maya then put her empty bowl of noodles away. Soon, Maya and Maggie entered their rooms. Maya grabbed a towel and got ready to take a bath.

Around fifteen years later, the local city government decided— despite local fears—to build a bridge across the Stamtona River. This building of the bridge was later reported in a newspaper and as a result, more of the locals gained more confidence and became less fearful of the mysterious croco- dile. Even so, there were still a handful of residents that were afraid that something bad would happen.

One evening, Maya and Arnold were with their family at their parents' house, reading about the new bridge in the newspaper. Their parents were out and about shopping, while Arnold, Maya, and their families stayed at their house. It was Christmas, and Arnold was setting up a Christmas tree. Maggie had already moved away and had her own family. Maya and

Arnold each had their own family, however they visited their parents' every holiday. It was a large family gathering.

"Wow, look at that!" Maya said. "They finally built a bridge."

"That's great to hear," Arnold replied. "Maybe we can drive back home using the new bridge, since it's faster."

"That's a great idea! By the way, it says that the bridge will be supported from the banks of the river, not built with supports in the river. I guess that's just in case the mysterious crocodile is real."

"I guess so, but I still believe that it's superstition."

"Well, we'll find out."

HUNTING ENCOUNTERS

I

Double Brother

O nce upon of time, there was a twenty-two-year-old young man named Christopher. He was married to a twenty-year-old girl named Kelly. They lived nearby a forest in a semi-rural location where his parents and his fifteen-year-old brother, Jerry, lived. Christopher and Jerry were both very handsome guys. They both had short and curly hair. Christopher was mostly nonchalant, not chatty, and very outgoing. Jerry, on the other hand, was very energetic, extremely outgoing, clever, and liked to be independent. They both enjoyed doing hobbies.

Christopher lived next to his parents' house. They lived far from the city, around fifty miles away. They lived in the small town of Bitterfruit; however, the people didn't live close to each other.

Christopher liked hunting, and so did his brother. They also worked in a farm. Their parents taught the brothers how to hunt ever since they were little. Besides hunting, they cut and collected wood and then they sold it at a market nearby. All of the houses were made of wood, along with the floor. Each house had a big backyard and also a garden.

Christopher's house was not that big. It had only two bedrooms, one bathroom, one living room, one kitchen, and one dining room. His parents' house was slightly bigger. Christopher's wife, Kelly, was very nice. She had long, straight hair. She was laid-back, a bit chatty, and outgoing, similar to Christopher. She loved to clean up the house and cook. The house was always sparkling clean because of this. They had been married for almost a year. She was a few months pregnant.

On a late afternoon in summer, Kelly was craving for some raw honey from a tree. Christopher was cutting wood outside when she approached him.

"I'm craving for some raw honey. I think it is because of the baby." While she was speaking, she was rubbing her belly. "Do you know where to get some?"

Christopher smiled. "I will do whatever I got to do. I will go hunting in the forest and get honey. I will bring Jerry with me."

"Good idea," she said. "He likes hunting. Do you want me to get him?"

"No, I'll go get him and tell my Mom and Dad."

Kelly went back inside, and Christopher went to his parents' house. Both of his parents were sitting at the front porch, enjoying the sun.

Christopher approached them. "Mom, Dad, where is Jerry?"

His father, Edward, said, "He's inside the house."

"He's in his room," said his mother, Eliza. "What's going on?"

"Nothing is going on. I just thought I'd ask him something."

Christopher entered his parents' house and called out for his brother.

"Jerry, Jerry!"

Jerry came out from his room. "I'm here. What's going on?"

"Hey, would you like to come with me to do some hunting?"

"Sure! Now?"

"Yes, now."

"Great, give me five minutes, I will get ready."

"Okay, I will get ready, too. When you are done, call for me. I will be at my house."

Jerry replied, "Okay."

Jerry then got dressed, picked up his backpack, and placed a few items in it, including water. He also grabbed his bow and some arrows before leaving the house.

"Where are you going, Son?" asked Edward.

"Are you going hunting?" Eliza asked before he could respond. "It's almost late."

Christopher, who'd gotten ready quicker than expected, had decided to walk back to meet his brother. He too had a backpack and a bow and some arrows. He heard his parents question Jerry and decided to jump in.

"We won't be too long, Mom. I'm taking him hunting. I'm also gonna get honey for Kelly. She's craving for raw honey."

"Oh, okay then," Eliza said. "Don't be too late."

"Yes," said Edward, "And be careful out there."

"Hey, keep your brother by your side!" Eliza said.

Christopher laughed and held up his hands. "Okay, bye Mom, bye Dad."

Jerry then said, "Bye Mom, bye Dad!"

"Watch out for wild animals, Jerry," said his dad.

"Stay with your big brother," said his mother.

"Okay, okay, I will."

The brothers walked off towards the forest. Ten minutes later, they both entered the forest, and almost right away, Jerry spotted something.

"Christopher, look, it's a deer."

"Oh yeah, do you want to shoot it?"

"Yeah, I'll take it."

Jerry got his bow ready, pulled out an arrow, and aimed for the deer. He took the shot, but he missed. The deer got spooked and ran into the dense forest.

"Wait here," Christopher said. "I'm going after it."

Christopher ran after the deer. However, after around an hour of waiting, Christopher still hadn't come. Jerry was getting worried. He was pacing back and forth, thinking about why his big brother was taking so long. He started wondering if something terrible happened. He picked up his bag and quickly went to his brother's house.

As he approached, he called out. "Kelly, Kelly!"

Kelly came out. "Hey Jerry, where's Christopher?"

"I don't know, he's in the forest. He went after a deer and hasn't returned."

Edward and Eliza then soon came by, after hearing the commotion outside.

"Hey, what's going on?" said Edward.

"Christopher is in the forest," Jerry said. "Something might be wrong."

They all soon went out to the edge of the forest. But before they had a chance to enter, Christopher emerged.

"Hey," he said, "what are you guys doing here? Hi Kelly, I got your honey. I didn't get the deer, though."

"We were worried about you," Edward said.

"Yes, Christopher," Eliza said. "We were just about to go in the forest to look for you!"

Christopher looked puzzled. "Well, I'm fine."

"That's alright," Kelly said. "I'm glad you're here and safe."

"I was getting worried," Jerry said. "I thought something bad happened."

Kelly was about to give Christopher a hug, when all of a sudden, another person emerged from the forest—another person who looked just like Christopher.

"Sorry, couldn't catch the deer. I got some honey for Kelly, however."

They were all shocked and confused.

"How are there two of you?!" Kelly said. "Who's my real husband!?"

One of them said, "I am!"

The other said, "No, I am."

They started arguing. They were getting ready to fight each other when Jerry stopped them.

"Okay, here's the deal. I'm going to find out who's real and who's not."

Kelly was upset. "What are we going to do now? There are two Christophers!"

Edward then had an idea.

"Ask them questions that only the real Christopher would know the answer to."

"Yeah," said Eliza. "That will work!"

"Great idea!" Jerry said. "Kelly, you should start."

Kelly thought for a moment. "What's my favorite food?"

Both of them replied at the same time. "Chicken Pot Pie!"

"Okay, what's my favorite color?"

Both answered, "Pink!"

Eliza turned to the others. "This doesn't appear to be working."

"Here," said Jerry, "let me a try one. What's my favorite activity?"

Again, they both replied. "Hunting!"

Jerry then tried a more difficult question.

"What's the color of my favorite shirt?"

One of them replied, "Yellow!"

The other replied, "Blue!"

Then, they started arguing about what the color of the shirt is until Jerry stopped them.

"You're both wrong, it is red!"

"Let's call the police," Edward said. "This is not working."

"No, no, no," said Jerry. "That won't work. What are the police going to do, put them both in jail?"

Jerry started thinking. Promptly, he came up with an idea. He reached into his bag.

"What are you doing, Jerry?" Kelly asked.

"I have an idea, just bear with me!"

"What are you going to do, Son?" Edward asked.

"I think he knows," said Eliza.

Jerry then took out a bottle and poured the water out.

Kelly looked at him, puzzled. "What are you going to do with that bottle?"

"Yes dear," said Eliza, "what are you going to do with that?"

"Trust me," he said. "This will work."

Jerry then went up to the Christophers who had fallen to arguing with each other.

One said, "Get out of here, you're the fake!" The other said, "No, you're clearly the fake one!"

"Hey," yelled Jerry, "quiet, you two!"

They both stopped arguing.

Then Jerry said, "If you're my real brother, you can fit in this bottle."

One of the Christophers just glared at him. "Jerry, I can't fit in that bottle, but I'm your real brother!"

The other smirked. "I'm your real brother, Jerry. Look, I can easily fit in that bottle."

"Okay," said Jerry, "go ahead if you're my real brother."

Kelly, Edward, and Eliza were confused as to what Jerry was doing; however, they kept watching. Immediately, one of the Christophers entered the bottle. As soon as he entered, Jerry got a cap for the bottle and shut the bottle tight.

The fake Christopher started shouting from inside the bottle. "*Hey, let me out! I'm Kelly's husband! Kelly, it's true!*"

Jerry turned back to the others. "See? I know what I'm doing."

He then directed his attention to the spirit in the bottle. "So, why are you imitating my brother? Do you want to be my brother?"

"*Because your brother is Kelly's husband! I want to be Kelly's husband! I don't want to be your brother.*"

"Oh, you're evil," said Jerry. "Good to know, you're trapped now!"

Kelly overheard and shuddered. "Oh, it's an evil being! Don't let it out!"

The spirit said, "*Okay, okay, I'm sorry! Let me out!*"

Christopher walked up and clapped his brother on the shoulder. "Thanks, Brother, for helping me out."

"Great thinking, Jerry!" Edward said. "I'm proud of you! How did you figure it out?"

"I used to watch supernatural shows. I knew spirits could change shape, so I thought I might as well give it a try."

Everybody then started laughing.

"Oh, I get it now!" Kelly said. "That's genius!"

Christopher said, "Genius, indeed!"

"Great job, Son!" Edward said.

"Jerry is so smart!" Eliza said. "He stopped that evil spirit in its tracks!"

"Thanks, Mom and Dad!"

Christopher then hugged Jerry, then Kelly, then his parents. Then Christopher looked at the spirit in the bottle.

"Keep him there," he said. "Let's get rid of him."

"Yeah," said Jerry. "Let's get rid of this imposter."

Christopher picked up the bottle, and he threw it back into the forest. The fake Christopher started screaming as the bottled sailed out of sight. *"Let me out! Nooo…"*

Then the brothers, along with their family, headed back to their houses, and the spirit was never heard from again.

2

Jerry & Layla

It was fifteen years later, and Jerry was now around thirty years old. After he finished college, he moved away from his parents and his brother to a different town called Jungletown. It was forty miles away from his parents' house. He used to have a job there, but he quit his job and opened his own business where he worked for himself. He lived by himself, using the money he'd earned to buy his own house, farm, and garden. He still enjoyed hunting once in a while. He also always tried to maintain contact with his parents, either by visiting or calling them.

One evening, he visited his parents after he got off from work early. He knocked on their door.

"Who is it?" Edward asked from the living room where he was watching TV.

"It's me, Jerry."

Edward got up and opened the door. "Oh, come on in, Son!"

"Thanks Dad. Where is Mom?"

"She's in the kitchen. So, how are you doing, Jerry?"

"I'm doing well, Dad. How are you and Mom doing?"

"We're doing fine."

Then, Edward called back to the kitchen. "Eliza, Eliza, Jerry is here."

Eliza, taken by surprise. "Jerry?" Then she quickly came out and gave her youngest son a hug. "Oh, my boy, how was work?"

"It was alright."

"Jerry, m'boy," Edward said, "when are you gonna get in a relationship and get married?"

Jerry smiled. "Soon Dad, but not now."

"Yeah Jerry, when are you gonna get married?" Eliza said. "You're thirty years old now. You're very handsome, a lot of pretty girls like you. You've got a good education, you got your own house, and even your own business. What are you waiting for? You can get any girl you want."

"I'm trying to find the *right* girl, Mom."

Edward placed his hand on Jerry's shoulder. "Come on Jerry, what kind of girl do you want?"

"I don't know, Dad. I'm not finding one that is fit for me yet, that's all."

"Are you gonna stay for dinner?" Eliza asked.

"Sorry, Mom, I can't. I have a few errands to do. I just wanted to see how you guys were doing."

Eliza turned to Edward. "Isn't that nice?"

"Thank you for visiting us, Son," Edward said.

"Alright," said Jerry. "I have to leave now. Bye Mom, bye Dad."

"Y'know, if you're too busy, you can always call us," Eliza said. "I only wish you could stay for dinner."

"Some other time, Mom."

Eliza looked a little disappointed. "Okay, take care, Son."

"You're not going to see your brother?" Edward asked.

"I will next time, Dad. Just tell him I said hello and that I couldn't stay since I'm in a hurry. I will see him next time."

"Okay, take care," Edward said.
"You too Dad, bye."
Then Jerry left. Eliza closed the door.

On a Friday night, he had a dream. In the dream, he ate a piece of venison, it was very tender and delicious. He slept late, and when he woke up next morning, he decided this was his brain telling him to go hunting. And so later in the early afternoon, he went out into a nearby forest with his bow and arrow. He went deep into the forest. He didn't find any deer and he started to get tired. He found a big rock, and then decided to take a rest on the rock. And since he had slept late that day, he soon fell fast asleep once more.

When he got up, he heard a noise from nearby. He looked around to find out where the noise was coming from. Then he saw five, very pretty girls. They were taking a bath and swimming in a lake nearby. He was wondering who they could be, and why they were in the middle of a dense forest far from any neighborhoods. Therefore, he started hiding behind the big rock. He thought that he should marry one of those girls, but he didn't know how.

Then he saw their clothes were lying on the side of the lake. He noticed that there were wings on the clothes. It turned out that they were not regular girls—these were instead angels. These angels couldn't use all of their magical powers without their clothes.

Jerry didn't know this, of course.

Despite that, he came up with an idea. He decided that the angels couldn't fly without their clothes, because their wings were on them, so Jerry tried to find a stick to reach in and pick up one of the girls' clothes. He then decided to use an arrow he was carrying instead. He snagged one set of clothes and snuck home and hid them in his barn. When he returned to the glade by the lake, he saw four girls flying away into the sky—and one girl crying in the lake.

He came up upon her. "What's going on?"

"My clothes are gone! I cannot return to my home."

"Where's your home?"

"High in the sky," she said. "I can't go back without my clothes."

"Oh, I'm so sorry."

Jerry took off his shirt and gave it to her, pretending to be a hero.

"Thank you," she said. "I really appreciate it."

Then she came out from the water. The angel was really pretty. Her eyes were like diamonds. Her skin was as smooth as a baby's bottom. Her hair was wavy, shiny, and long.

"Who are you?" she asked.

"My name is Jerry, I live nearby here. What's your name?"

"My name is Layla."

"What are you doing here?"

"I was just out taking a bath in this lake with my friends, until my clothes disappeared."

"The other four were your friends?" he asked.

"Yes, those were my friends. I'm the youngest out of them."

"Oh, I see now. Do you want to come with me to my house?"

"Okay," she said.

"Come on, it's not far."

They headed to Jerry's house.

When they got to the house, Jerry handed Layla a towel and gave her dry clothes for her to wear. It was late afternoon.

"Are you hungry?" he asked.

"No, I'm fine. Thank you."

Jerry went to the kitchen and boiled water then made some tea for himself and Layla. Layla looked around the house. The house looked surprisingly clean and neat. The house wasn't big, as it only had two bedrooms, one bathroom, a kitchen, and a living room. Most of the house was made out of wood, including the floor. There was a barn next to the house. There was also a garden around the house, and it was located far from any neighborhoods.

"Well, make yourself comfortable," Jerry said.

"Okay, thank you."

Then, Jerry came out from the kitchen and handed her a cup of tea.

"What is this?" she asked.

"A cup of tea." Jerry replied. Jerry then thought to himself, *"Could it be that she'd never had tea before?"*

"Thank you," she said. "You're so kind."

Jerry felt a little guilty. "Don't mention it."

Then, Jerry put down his tea.

"Come on, I'll show you around."

Layla also put her cup down on a table and followed Jerry. They went to the back yard.

"This is my garden," he said. "It surrounds the house and is full of fruits and vegetables."

Layla was amazed. "Very nice, I love it."

"Over there," Jerry said as he pointed to his barn, "I have a barn with lots of wheat. When I want to make bread, I just grind the wheat and cook it."

Layla nodded. "Okay, that's a huge garden and a big barn."

Jerry looked at Layla and was struck by how beautiful she was. "Come on, I'll show you where the bathroom is and the room you can stay in."

They both entered the house, Jerry pointed out the bathroom and opened the bathroom door then turned the light on.

"This is the bathroom."

"Nice."

"Thank you."

Then Jerry entered one of the bedrooms.

"Here it is," he said. "Here is your room. If you want to
stay that is. Do you like it? Sorry, it's small."

"That's fine," she said. "It's small, but it's clean, and you're
really very kind for offering it to me. I like it."

She smiled at him, and again he felt guilty for having
trapped her on earth.

"If you feel tired, Layla, you can get some rest."

"Okay, thanks Jerry."

"No problem, if you're hungry I will fix you something
to eat."

"I'm fine right now, thank you though."

"Okay, whenever you're hungry just let me know."

"Okay, I will," Layla said.

From then on, Layla stayed with Jerry, since she had nowhere
else to go, and to her, Jerry seemed like a very nice young
man. Every day, when Jerry was working in the farm, garden,
or out in the forest hunting, Layla cooked for him. Whenever
he came home, the food was always ready and already had
been placed on the dining room table. A few weeks later, they
both fell in love. Jerry then took her to Bitterfruit to meet his
parents and his brother's family.

When they arrived, he knocked on the door of his parents'
house. Eliza then came and opened the door.

"Jerry! I'm glad you came to visit! And I see you brought your new girlfriend?"

"Yes," he said proudly. "This is Layla, my girlfriend. We're going to get married."

"Oh," Eliza said, surprised. "That's wonderful! Come on in, come on in!"

Edward then came.

"Look, Edward," said Eliza, "it is Jerry and his girlfriend, Layla! They're going to get married! Isn't that great?"

"Oh, I'm so happy that you finally got in a relationship, Son! I'm proud of you!"

Jerry then gave Eliza and Edward a hug. Layla also gave them a hug.

Eliza then said to Layla, "Make yourself at home!"

"Oh, thank you!"

Jerry sat down in a chair with Layla.

"Do you know if Christopher and his family are at home?"

"I think they're at home," Eliza said. "Let's get them here."

Eliza went out to Christopher's house, and a few minutes later, she was back with Christopher and his family.

"Oh hey, little Brother! I'm glad to see you again."

"Hey Christopher, I'm happy to see you."

Jerry then saw Christopher's fourteen-year-old daughter.

"Oh, Ariel, you are looking great!"

"Thanks, Uncle Jerry."

Jerry then gave Ariel a hug.

Jerry then turned back to his brother and sister-in-law. "Sorry I've haven't been around much guys. I've been busy."

"Oh, it's no problem," Kelly said. "At least you visit us when you can."

"Hey Jerry," said Christopher, looking at Layla. "I see you have a girlfriend."

"Oh yes, meet Layla."

Layla said, "Hi, nice to meet you."

"Nice to meet you, too. I'm Jerry's older brother, Christopher."

Kelly approached, and shook Layla's hand. "And I'm Kelly. It's so nice to meet you."

"Nice to meet you, too," Layla said.

"We're going to get married." said Jerry all of a sudden.

"Oh wow," said Kelly. "When's the big date?"

"We're planning to get married next week," Jerry said.

Eliza was shocked. "Really? Next week? That's very soon!"

"Well, Mom," said Jerry, "we've known each other for a while, now."

"Well, you never told *us*," she said. "We are meeting Layla for the first time."

"I know, Mom. I'm sorry. I didn't tell you because we didn't have plans to get married, yet."

Eliza still seemed perplexed by the rush. "Well, now that we know, we will help you with anything you need."

"Thank you, Mom. We're not going to have a big celebration," he said. "We're just going to have a simple wedding."

"How come?" asked Kelly.

"Layla doesn't want a big celebration," Jerry said. "Isn't that right, Honey?"

"Oh," said Layla. "Yes, that's right."

"I see," said Kelly.

Eliza then said, "Oh, it's almost dinner time! I'm going to cook for everybody, we can all have dinner together."

Jerry replied, "Okay, that sounds great."

So, they soon all had dinner together. However, Jerry and Layla had to leave early, since they had many errands to do.

"Sorry guys, we have to go to do some errands. Are you going to come to our wedding?"

"Of course," Christopher said.

"Okay," said Jerry then turned to Ariel. "Come here, you!"

He gave her a big hug. "I'll miss you, make sure to listen to your mom and dad."

"Okay, bye Uncle Jerry"

"Bye, Ariel."

Layla gave Eliza and Kelly a hug. "Goodbye!"

"Bye, Layla. It was nice meeting you!"

Jerry and Layla then exited the house.

Edward closed the door and turned to his wife. "What do you think about Jerry's girlfriend?"

"She's the prettiest girl I ever saw in my life."

"I think so too," said Edward.

A week later, Jerry and Layla went to a local church in Bitterfruit for their wedding. Jerry's parents, and Christopher's family, along with a few others, mostly church members, were all there.

Eliza approached Jerry and pulled him aside. "Where's Layla's family?"

Jerry softly replied, "Oh, I forgot to tell you, Mom. She's by herself. Her parents aren't here."

"Oh, I see," said Eliza.

Eliza then told Edward, Christopher, and Christopher's family about it. They didn't seem disappointed. Jerry then went back to Layla. Everybody looked at Layla with amazement, thinking she was one of the most beautiful girls they ever saw. Some started whispering to each other on how beautiful she was. Jerry and Layla stood in front of everybody. After a couple minutes, the pastor pronounced them husband and wife. They then both had their first kiss. Everybody then started clapping with a few cheers. The pastor then gave a couple closing remarks, and then the wedding ended. Soon, everybody left.

A week later, after getting married, Jerry was coming home from work. Before he entered the house, he went to check the barn. Before he got married, he always supplied the barn with more wheat. However, after getting married, he stopped, since the barn was already full. When he entered it, the barn was still full of wheat. Jerry was confused, as he thought the barn would have had less wheat. He knew that Layla loved cooking, and so he thought this was very odd. However, since he couldn't believe that the barn was still the same, he thought it was just his eye playing tricks on him, so he disregarded it.

Two weeks later, like before, he checked on the barn, again. Once again, the barn was still full, and it in fact had more wheat stored in it than before. This caught him completely off guard, and this time he didn't think it was just his eyes playing tricks. He still didn't say anything to his wife, however.

The next day, he managed to get off work early. Layla was cooking dinner and was about to go to the garden to get something.

"Oh, you're home early. I'm going to go to the garden to get something. Don't open the oven."

Jerry thought this had to do something with the barn, and it being always full. Even though she told him not to, he decided to open the oven in order to see what's going on. However, he hesitated, since he knows that his wife told him not to. Eventually he opened the oven, and what he saw shocked him. He saw a single grain of wheat in the oven. Layla came back in and saw that Jerry opened the oven.

Layla then got upset. "I told you not to open the oven!"

Jerry was confused. "But I don't understand. What are you cooking? That's only a small grain of wheat!"

"That's how I cook, Jerry! Now, I can't cook that way anymore."

"I'm sorry," Jerry said. "I didn't know."

Jerry then realized that Layla had magical powers, unlike a regular human being. From then on, Layla had to cook normally. She had to turn the wheat into grain and grind it then cook it. From then on, she had to do this every day.

Despite this happening, they were still happily married, and a year later, Layla gave birth to a baby girl. They named her Rachiel. Over time, the wheat pile got smaller and smaller until finally, one day when Rachiel was three months old and two weeks after they visited their parents for Thanksgiving, she found her clothes hidden in the barn beneath the wheat when she was about to cook dinner.

She was then shocked, for now she knew that it had been Jerry who'd taken her clothes on that day she'd been bathing with her friends. Layla ran into the house with the clothes and rushed towards Jerry who was holding Rachiel and confronted him.

"It was you. You took my clothes!? And you hid them in your barn."

Jerry was frightened. "I'm very sorry, Layla! I love you, though!"

"I'm sorry, Jerry," she said. "But I can't stay with you. I have to go back to my kingdom."

Jerry started crying. "But, what about our baby?"

Layla started crying, too. "Build a shed near the house, every night put Rachiel in a bassinet then leave her there in the shed. I will come to visit and feed her every night, but no peeking. And if she gets married, have her wear my wedding dress."

Layla then put on her clothes and gave a kiss to Rachiel. "Goodbye, Jerry."

She then flew away.

He fell to his knees, weeping, with Rachiel in arms. "No, please come back!"

The next day, Jerry built a small shed out back and he put Rachiel in a bassinet and then left her there overnight. Layla came every night to visit and feed Rachiel, and Jerry never took a peek. Since Layla was gone, Jerry almost never visited his parents. He just occasionally called them to check in on them. However, he always tried to prevent them from finding out the truth, since he was too afraid to tell them, believing that they would be disappointed in him. This continued until Rachiel reached a year old and started to walk.

After that, Jerry stopped putting the baby in the shed. He then turned the shed into a garage, and Layla never visited them again. A few days later, Jerry visited his parents along with Rachiel. Jerry knocked on the door of his parents' house.

"Hello, anybody home? It's me, Jerry."

Eliza opened the door. "Hello Jerry, come on in!"

Jerry and Rachiel came in.

"Oh, Rachiel," said Eliza, "you're a big girl now! I haven't seen you in almost a year!"

"Yes, she is," said Jerry. "I'm sorry that we couldn't visit more."

"Is Rachiel learning how to walk and talk?"

"Yeah, she took her first steps a couple days ago."

"Oh, that's wonderful! She's so cute and loveable!"

Edward then came out to the living room, but before he could even greet his son and granddaughter, Jerry spoke.

"By the way, I need help taking care of Rachiel. Layla and I are going to go to travel to a different state for a business job. I can't find a babysitter, since this is very urgent."

This didn't make sense to Eliza, but of course, a lot about Jerry and Layla hadn't made sense to her recently.

"Oh okay," she said. "Well, we'll be happy to help take care of Rachiel. Where *is* Layla, by the way?"

Jerry could tell his mother was suspicious, and he couldn't meet her gaze.

"She's packing our stuff at home to get ready for our trip."

"Well," Eliza said, trying to sound casual. "She sounds like a very busy person."

"Yes," said Jerry. "She works really hard to assist me in taking care of business, the house, and our farm."

Edward too sounded confused and dubious. "Hey Son, don't worry about Rachiel. We'll make sure to take good care of her."

Jerry could barely look at them. "Thanks Mom and Dad. I have to go now. I'll call you and send some money every month, until I'm able to pick up Rachiel."

"Alright, Son," Edward said. "Take care."

Before leaving, Jerry bent down and gave Rachiel a goodbye kiss.

Eliza bent down and scooped up her granddaughter. "Wave goodbye to your daddy, Rachiel. Goodbye, Jerry. Take care."

Six months later, Jerry became the Mayor of Jungletown. Around that time, he met a guy named David, a local government worker, and the two ended up becoming friends. David's wife had passed away, and he had a little boy named Freddy, who was about Rachiel's age. David developed a drinking problem after the death of his wife, and so he lost his job soon after he met Jerry. He was unable to pay for his house and got kicked out. Because of all of his troubles, he was unable to effectively take care of Freddy. But he didn't want the state to take away Freddy from him.

One day, David and Freddy were visiting Jerry. Freddy had brought a toy car from home, and while they were there, David saw the way Jerry was smiling as he watched the boy playing with it. That gave David an idea.

"Jerry, do you mind adopting my son? I can't take care of him anymore, and you're the only person I can trust with him."

Jerry was surprised, but he made a quick decision. "Sure, David. Besides, Rachiel needs a close friend. You can still visit Freddy anytime you want, since I know you care for him a lot. Just focus on getting yourself together, don't worry about Freddy. I will make sure to take good care of him."

After Jerry adopted Freddy, the boy came to live with him, but David still visited occasionally. Besides, David didn't live that far from Jerry's house.

One night, about two months after Jerry became mayor of Jungletown, Edward, Eliza, and Rachiel were settling in to watch their favorite TV show in their home in Bitterfruit. They'd barely heard from Jerry since he dropped off Rachiel.

At this point, their granddaughter was about almost two years old.

"I know I've said it before, Edward," said Eliza, "but I can't understand why Layla never calls here. It's only ever Jerry who calls, and not very often, and he never has any news about her."

"I know," said Edward. "It's a bit weird. Something could be wrong."

"Doesn't she want to check on her baby?"

Edward nodded gravely. "Well, I hope nothing bad happened."

"It doesn't sound right," Eliza continued. "It has been eight months since Jerry dropped Rachiel here."

"I know, dear but—"

There was an unexpected knock at the door.

Eliza went to the door. "Who is it?"

"It's me, Jerry."

"Oh!" she said. "Come on in, Jerry. We were just talking about you and Layla."

Jerry and Freddy entered the house. Jerry ignored his mother's last comment.

"Mom," he said, "I want you to meet my adopted son, Freddy."

This was the first time she'd hear about Freddy. He looked to be about a year older than Rachiel. Probably around three, she thought.

"Oh, hi, how are you doing, sweetie?"

Freddy replied, "Hi. I'm doing okay."

"Hi Jerry," said Edward who'd got up and joined them. "How are you doing?"

"Hi Dad, I'm doing great. How are you doing?"

"As usual, doing fine."

"Meet my son, Freddy, Dad."

"You have a son?" Edward was as confused as Eliza.

"Adopted son, Edward," she said.

"Oh."

"Isn't he handsome, dear?"

"He sure is," Edward said.

Eliza put on a bright smile. "Jerry got a pretty girl and a handsome boy."

"Thank you, Mom," Jerry said.

That's when Jerry saw Rachiel in front of the TV and slowly approached her.

"Rachiel, you are a big girl now!"

Rachiel quickly ran away towards her grandmother. She didn't recognize Jerry.

Jerry crouched so he wouldn't be as scary and spoke in a soft voice.

"Rachiel, do you remember me? I'm your dad!"

Rachiel then looked at Eliza.

"He is your dad, Rachiel. Remember, he brought you here when you were a year old."

Rachiel looked at Jerry for a second then gave him a hug. Jerry was so happy, he almost started crying.

"Rachiel," he said. "Look, I also brought you a friend. He's only a little older than you are. His name is Freddy, and he's very friendly!"

Soon Rachiel and Freddy started playing together, and once they were occupied. Edward pulled his son aside. Enough was enough.

"Where is Layla?" he said.

"She is busy."

"Jerry," said Eliza, "I feel like you're hiding something. Is there something wrong?"

"Yes, what's going on?" Edward said. He sounded quite cross. "We're not stupid, and we deserve to know the truth."

That's when Jerry knew he had to come clean. He hung his head.

"I'm sorry Mom and Dad, I didn't tell you the truth because I didn't want you to be worried."

"Have you had a divorce, Jerry?" Eliza asked.

"No. Layla left two weeks after we visited here for Thanksgiving last time. Rachiel was only three months old."

"What!?" Eliza couldn't believe it. "I *knew* something was wrong. No wonder you didn't come for Christmas. Usually, you always come for holidays."

"Two weeks after your last visit?" Edward was annoyed with his son and had to be careful not to raise his voice because the kids would hear. "That was over a *year* ago!"

"I know. I know." said Jerry. "I'm sorry. It's a long story."

They were sitting in the dining room. "I will make tea," said Eliza.

As Eliza was boiling a pot of water, Edward tried to calm down. He looked at his son and took a deep breath.

"Come on, Jerry," he said, "tell us what happened. The *whole* story."

Jerry sighed. Then he proceeded to tell his parents the whole story, from how he first met her in the forest and hid her clothes in the barn, to how she ended up living with him. He talked about how they fell in love and got married and eventually had Rachiel. He told them about Layla's magical powers and how she ended up having to cook normally and visit the barn every day—and how one day she found the clothes he'd hidden there. Then he told them the saddest part of the story, about how Layla left him and the shed and the bassinet and her nightly visits. Finally, he told them about Layla's wish that Rachiel be married in her wedding dress.

By the time he had finished telling his story, Jerry was quite upset because it was hard for him to admit all that he had done wrong.

"Oh my goodness," Edward said. "First, Christopher has a doppelganger, now we find out that you married an angel and she left you. This is madness."

"You should have just told us the truth, Jerry," said Eliza.

"I didn't want you guys worrying."

"We *deserved* the truth, Jerry," Edward said. "We've raised Rachiel for the last eight months."

"I know, Dad. I'm sorry."

"Well," Edward said. "What *are* you doing now?"

"I'm the Mayor of Jungletown."

Eliza brightened. "That's a great job. It must be hard, though."

"Yeah, it is hard. However, I will be able to take care both of these kids with the money I'm making. I'm just glad that Rachiel is happy and that she has a friend, now."

Edward nodded. "Yes, they both look happy."

"So, now that you're mayor," Eliza said, "are you gonna get married, again?"

"No."

"Why *not?*" snapped Edward. "Don't you think those kids deserve a mother?"

Jerry flinched. "Okay maybe, but not now, Dad."

Eliza tried to change the subject. "You guys hungry?"

"No," said Jerry, "we already ate."

"You guys are going to stay, aren't you?" Edward said, but it sounded more like a command than a question. "It has been eight months since you came here."

"Yes, Dad," Jerry said. "Yes, we're gonna stay for a few days."

"Oh that's good," Eliza said, "Christopher and Kelly have been asking about you, too. We've all been concerned for quite some time."

"I know. And I'm sorry," Jerry replied, "Yeah, I want to see them again too, of course. Are they at home now?"

"No," said Edward. "They are out of town."

"But they will be back tomorrow," Eliza said.

"Oh, okay." Jerry sounded tired and sad.

"I will fix your bed so you can get some rest," Eliza said. "There's an extra bed in Rachiel's room that Freddy can take."

"Thanks Mom."

Next morning, Christopher and his family arrived home. Jerry was still in his bed. Eliza was in the kitchen cooking breakfast. Edward was in the backyard, feeding the chickens and collecting eggs. Jerry's kids were still asleep. Jerry heard noises from outside his room. He then woke up. Jerry went outside and saw Christopher.

"Hey Christopher," he said. "How are you doing?"

Christopher was taken by surprise at the sight of his kid brother. "Oh hey, Jerry, how are you doing? When did you get here?"

"Yesterday, with my little boy."

"You have a little boy?" he said. "When did that happen?"

"I adopted him from my best friend so that Rachiel can have a friend to play with, and so that I can help take care of him."

"That's great," he said.

Then Christopher called for Kelly. "Kelly, Kelly, Jerry is here. He came yesterday."

Kelly came out, with her new baby in her arms. "Hi Jerry, how are you doing? Where is Layla?"

"She's not with me anymore."

Kelly was shocked. "Why?"

"She left a few months after Rachiel was born."

"I'm so sorry to hear that," she said.

"What happened?" asked Christopher.

"It's a long story," Jerry said. "Mom and Dad will tell you. You have a new baby?"

Kelly brightened. "Yeah, his name is Robby, he's about a month old."

"That's a nice name."

"Thank you," she said. "He's a sweet baby."

Jerry did the math in his head. "So, last time when we came here for Thanksgiving, you were already pregnant?"

Kelly nodded. "Yes, only about a two months along. We weren't telling anyone yet."

"Oh okay." Then Jerry reached out and held Robby's fingers. "Hi little guy, how are you doing?"

Robby didn't say anything.

"So how long are you planning to stay in town, Jerry?" Christopher asked.

"For a few more days."

"Good," he said. "That's good. We can catch up."

"What are you doing now Jerry?" Kelly asked.

"I'm actually the mayor back in Jungletown."

Kelly responded, "That's great!"

"Congratulations, Brother!"

Jerry smiled.

"And are you planning to get married again?" Christopher asked.

"No, not now."

"Come on, you got a good job."

Jerry nodded tiredly. "I know. And I will think about it."

Then Ariel came out. "Hi Uncle Jerry." She rushed over and gave him a hug. "How are you doing?"

"I'm doing great. How are you?"

"I'm great," she said.

Jerry said, "I'm glad to hear that."

"C'mon," Christopher said, "why don't you come in?"

"Yeah come on in," said Kelly. "We just got back from being out of town."

"I know, Mom and Dad told me. By the way, you guys can come over for lunch later; we can then have a lunch together."

Christopher and Kelly thought that sounded like a great idea.

Then they went back to their house.

"Come on Uncle," said Ariel, "let's get in the house."

"Not now, later. My kids are gonna wake up."

"How many kids do you have?"

"It's only two. I adopted one boy, named Freddy.

"Oh," she said. "I didn't know that you had another kid. Where is your wife?"

"Layla's gone."

"What? She's gone?"

"Yeah, it's a long story."

"Okay," she said. "Well, I gotta get back in the house see you later Uncle Jerry."

"See you Ariel."

Jerry went back to his parents' house. His kids were still sleeping. Eliza was done cooking, and Edward was done with his chores. Eliza came out from the kitchen.

"Hi Mom," he said. "I met Christopher and his family outside, they just got back from out of town. I didn't know that they had a new baby."

"Oh yeah," she said. "I forgot to tell you about that. By the way, breakfast is ready, and the kids are still asleep. Why don't you eat first or drink coffee with your father over there in the dining room."

"Thanks Mom, but I'm not hungry yet."

Then Edward called out for Jerry from the dining room.

"Come on here, Jerry, get your breakfast."

"Later Dad."

Soon the kids came out.

Jerry saw them smiling. "Hi guys, how are you guys doing?"

Freddy went towards Jerry, and Rachiel ran towards her grandmother.

"Come on guys," Eliza said. "Let's get you cleaned up. Then we can have breakfast, okay?"

Rachiel nodded.

"Okay Freddy," Jerry said. "Go with grandma to get cleaned up."

"Okay."

Eliza brought them to the bathroom and gave them a bath. Jerry then decided to go to the dining room to join his father and have a cup of coffee.

At noon Edward went next door to Christopher's house. He knocked, and soon Christopher opened the door.

"Hi Dad."

"Come over for a lunch," Edward said. "Bring your family. We are gonna have lunch together."

"Okay."

Soon Christopher and his family went over to Edward's house for lunch.

Kelly saw Rachiel and Freddy and gave them a warm smile. "Hi Rachiel."

"Hi."

Kelly turned to Freddy. "Hi little guy, what's your name?"

"Freddy."

"Nice to meet you, Freddy."

Freddy was holding Jerry's hand.

"How old is he?" Christopher asked.

"He's three."

Ariel crouched down. "Hi Rachiel, hi Freddy."

Freddy and Rachiel were just holding Jerry's hands. Eliza and Edward were busy preparing food for lunch.

"Ariel, why don't you go help your grandparents," Kelly said.

"Okay."

"You're still planning on staying a little longer aren't you, Jerry?" Christopher asked.

"Maybe for a few days."

"Yeah," said Kelly, "it has been a long time."

Then Eliza called, "Hey everybody, lunch is ready."

Everybody sat on the chairs at the dining room, ready to eat.

After finishing lunch, Kelly and Ariel helped Eliza clean up the table and wash dishes while Christopher was holding Robby on his lap, in the living room with Jerry, Edward, Rachiel, and Freddy. After Kelly and Ariel finished helping Eliza, they were ready to go home.

Kelly took the baby from Christopher. "Are you ready to go home?"

"Yes. By the way, Jerry, come over sometime and bring your kids."

"Okay," said Jerry. "I'll do that."

Then Christopher turned to his parents. "Thanks Mom, and Dad."

"No problem, Christopher," said Edward.

"You're welcome," said Eliza.

After the rest of the adults said their goodbyes, Ariel beckoned Rachiel and Freddy over to her.

"Come here you two, give me a hug."

Freddy and Rachiel gave Ariel a hug. Then they went to Christopher and Kelly and gave them a hug and kiss and said goodbye. Christopher and his family returned back to their house.

Later that afternoon, Jerry got a call from Jungletown.

"Hello, what's going on? I'm at my parents' house with my kids…"

A few minutes later he said, "Alright, I will be home in about a couple of hours. Okay, see you there."

Jerry then hung up the phone and found his parents in the living room.

"Mom, Dad, I just got called, something important came up, and I have to get back. It's the part of being a mayor that I don't like. I have to be ready to respond when something comes up."

"We understand," Eliza said, though she looked disappointed. "Okay then, I will help you to get ready. Help me, Edward!"

Edward reluctantly got to his feet. "Righto."

"Thanks, Mom and Dad."

Edward and Eliza helped pack Rachiel's stuff and helped Rachiel and Freddy to get dressed. Soon there were all ready to go. There was a large bag with Rachiel's things that she had accumulated over the past eight months. She was sad to be going.

"Thanks Mom and Dad," said Jerry. "Come visit us sometimes. Bring Christopher and his family if you feel uncomfortable making the long trip on your own."

"Sure Jerry," said Edward, "that would be nice."

"We will visit you too, sometimes," Jerry said because he could tell that his mother would miss Rachiel a great deal.

"If you're too busy," Eliza said, "just give us a call so I can talk to my grandkids, I will be happy."

"Alright, Mom," said Jerry. "I promise, but we have to go now."

Then Rachiel and Freddy gave Edward a hug and then said goodbye.

"Bye, Grandpa," said Freddy.

Edward responded, "Goodbye Freddy and Rachiel, listen to your father, okay?"

"Yes," said Eliza to the children, "You two sweethearts behave yourselves."

"Okay," said Freddy.

Then, Jerry picked up Rachiel and balanced her on his hip as he walked next door to Christopher's place.

Ariel opened the door and could tell at a glance what was going on.

"Uncle Jerry, where are you going?"

"Home," he said. "Back to Jungletown."

"I thought you were gonna stay longer."

"I know. Unfortunately, I just got a call, something important came up."

"Oh, okay."

Ariel saw Rachiel and Freddy and smiled at them.

"You are all dressed up, looking so pretty and handsome."

"Are your parents home, Ariel?"

"I'll get them."

Christopher and Kelly were in the kitchen with their baby. They all came out.

"Jerry," Christopher said, "are you leaving?"

"Has something happened?" asked Kelly.

"We have to go, unfortunately. Mayoral business. I just got a call, and something important has come up. Maybe some other time we can stay longer, when I don't have so much work."

They understood, but Jerry could tell they were disappointed, especially Christopher. After everyone had said their goodbyes, Christopher walked them to Jerry's car.

"You take care of yourself, little Brother," he said. "And take care of these kids too."

"I will," Jerry said. "Hey, feel free to come visit us sometime. Bring your family, and mom and dad, at least when you can, and if possible."

"Okay, we will," said Christopher.

They all got in the car. Freddy and Rachiel sat beside each other in two car seats. Then Edward, Eliza, Christopher and his family waved at them and blew a kiss goodbye. Rachiel saw them in the window and did the same back to them. Freddy waved goodbye, as well. Jerry saw them do so in the rearview mirror and waved back at them and also blew a kiss. Soon, Jerry drove away.

Freddy and Rachiel grew up together. Jerry taught Freddy how to hunt with a bow and arrow and eventually how to run a farm. Jerry also taught Rachiel how to work in a farm and prepare food from the barn. Freddy grew up to become a handsome young man, and Rachiel grew up to become a beautiful young girl. Rachiel eventually got married with somebody she met in college, while Freddy stayed unmarried for a while.

However, one thing persisted: Rachiel always wondered where Layla was.

Jerry stuck with the falsehood that Layla had simply left without warning and that he didn't know where she was. He was soon faced with a dilemma, however; since Rachiel wanted Layla to come to her wedding, and she was determined to look for her mother, until she found her.

Jerry had no choice but to tell the truth.

"Rachiel, your mother left when you were one years old. She left to heaven. She wasn't a regular human being. She was an angel. I'm sorry that I haven't revealed this fact to you for all these years. But, here's the bright side: You are part-angel, and your beauty is taken from her. She wanted you to wear her wedding dress. And just maybe, she will visit you."

And she eventually did.

One evening, the day before Rachiel's wedding, Layla came to see Rachiel. It was a very sudden and surprising visit. She came to Rachiel's room when she was by herself, trying to put on her mother's wedding dress.

"Rachiel," she said. "I'm Layla, your mother. I heard that you were going to get married tomorrow. By the way, you look amazing."

Rachiel was shocked, yet happy. "Thank you, Mom. Why can't you stay here?"

"I'm sorry that I had to leave this world," Layla said. "This is not my home; my home is in the sky. I just simply can't live here. However, I always will love you."

Rachiel then gave Layla a big hug.

Before she left, Layla decided to give Rachiel a small gift. It was a soft, white, and silk scarf.

"If you have any trouble," Layla said, "you can wear this. All the trouble will end."

"Thank you, mother. I love you."

"I will always watch over you. Goodbye, sweetie."

Layla then swiftly left.

After both Freddy and Rachiel finished college, Freddy decided to pursue becoming a successful farmer and running his own big farm, and Rachiel decided to move away with her husband. Christopher and his family continued living nearby his parents. Ariel and Robby, meanwhile, grew up to become highly educated individuals, eventually moving away from their parents, buying their own houses, and doing their own thing in the city.

Edward and Eliza eventually passed away, but before they did, they continued living together nearby Christopher. Jerry and his family sometimes visited them, and they sometimes visited Jerry and his family. Jerry, at first, decided to live with Freddy. However, when Freddy got married and was able to work alone, he retired and moved in with Rachiel's family, living happily and peacefully until the day he died. Christopher and his wife decided to stay in their house and live together until they also passed away.

Afterword

All of these stories are based on both true stories and also legends. All of the characters are modernized, along with the setting. Every setting is based in the United States of America; however; these stories didn't take place in a modern time or in the United States of America. These stories all happened in the past, and they all happened in Indonesia.

"A Different Well" is based on a true story of an actual well that still exists today in Ungaran, Indonesia. The well's water did actually help people and cure ailments that would normally be incurable, and businesses did begin to appear nearby. However, it is also true that in modern times, the well is not how it was originally. This all happened in the late 1980s. Some people still believe today that the well works, as long as you believe in it and have good intentions. However, some things are not true. For example, the story about the boy smiling in is not necessarily true. It's simply a story based on a possibility that it could have happened. Some of the town names are based on real town names, along with the towns themselves. Scarcetree is based on the Indonesian town called Samarang, which translates as *scarce tamarind*. Since tamarind is a type of tree, the name was changed to simply Scarcetree. Newtown is based on a town called Ungaran. It loosely translates to something like *new settlement.* Green Mountain is a made-up name for the village where the well was located. Hillside is also a made-up name for the town where the character Lisa lives. Dogwood is a made-up name; however, the city is based off of the real city of Pati in Indonesia. All the towns are based on their real-life counterparts, but modernized somewhat, making them more like American towns. The characters are all based on real people, simply with different names. The well at Lisa's house is mostly unrelated to the actual, magical well, but it is included since it gives a good entry to the story.

"Bizarre Reptiles" are also based on true stories (with the second chapter being possibly a true story or simply a local legend), the setting is modernized and based in America, and the characters are based off of real people. The first story was actually shown in a newspaper, with an actual picture. It was a crocodile, however, instead of an alligator. The other story was based off of stories shared by others, where the fisherman told somebody, and the person told the main characters. These stories happened in the late 1990s, also in Indonesia. The city of Victorious is based off of Jakarta in Indonesia. Jakarta translates to *victorious city.* The name for the town of Green Valley is made up. The Stamtona River is based off of an actual river called Kali Silungonggo (locally known as Kali Gedhe, with Gedhe meaning *large*) near a village called Ngastorejo. Kali means *river.* The name "Stamtona" was chosen at random. It's not clear what Silungonggo translates to. The people in Ngastorejo do believe that the river is inhabited by a supernatural crocodile that wouldn't allow them to build a bridge over the river. However, it is possible that it is simply a myth or legend. Despite that, there are many stories about encounters with this supernatural crocodile, like the one in the story. People in Ngastorejo have finally built a simple suspension bridge over the Silungonggo River.

"**Hunting Encounters**" is based on Indonesian legends. The characters are based off of the characters in these legends. The setting has been modernized and altered so it fits with an American setting. The two stories are completely separate; however, they happened in the same era. These stories happened during the time of the Mataram Kingdom, when Indonesia—Java specifically—was ruled by kings and sultans. In the first story, it was originally just a husband and a wife. The husband didn't hunt, he just went to collect honey for his wife. The couple also had only one child. The person who resolved the problem was the King of Malowopati, named Dharmawasesa. There were no parents or brother involved. The Malowopati Kingdom and its king, Prabu Dharmawasesa, are possibly based off of the real Mataram Kingdom and its real king, Dharmawangsa. The town name, Bitterfruit, is a made-up name. The original name of the town is Bojonegoro, and it translates to *country relationship*. In the other story with Jerry, it's based off of the folktale/legend called "Jaka Tarub and the Seven Angels." Tarub is the name of the town where Jaka Tarub lived, which is a real, yet small, village that still exists today in Indonesia. Jaka means *bachelor* (a man who is not and has never been married). His original name is Kidang Telangkas. People called him Jaka Tarub because it was easier to call him by that than calling him by his real name. The original story had seven angels, while this adaption has five. The town name, Jungletown, is a made-up name. In the original story, the main character is a young man, who was adopted by a widow. His mother already passed away before he met the angels. He didn't have a brother, or any relatives, and the angel cooked rice instead of wheat. In addition to that, the angels wore shawls, with the shawls being the source of their magical powers. In this adaption, the angels wear stereotypical Christian angel clothes. On top of that, Jaka Tarub became a village chief instead of a town mayor. He then befriended the king of the Majapahit. In some retellings of the story, the son of the Majapahit was adopted, in others he wasn't and simply married Jaka Tarub's daughter. This story is said to have some relation to real life people in the history of Mataram. It is important to note that this story has many different types of alterations, just like any other myth. Despite that, the premise of the story stays the same in all of the alterations.